'*It will blow your*
'*This is a unique*
one like it'
'*I think it will be a*
'*You start looking*
'*A unique contribution to the pantheon of world literature*'

Radio BFBS

Much later, they were interrupted by a cock crowing outside the window. 'Thank you, my dear,' said the lord, who never stopped being a gentleman, and removed his suit, which he hadn't yet had time to do.

'Thank you!' said Titsiepoo, clutching his toe just in case he was thinking of jumping out of bed.

But she did not yet know the lord. 'I should like to be able to thank you again,' he said.

Titsiepoo closed her angelic eyes and let the lord do with her as he would. 'Thank you,' he said again, after a couple of hours.

Fiercely, Lord Crinkleton

PEGGY TAUB

Illustrated by the author

Sphere Books Limited

Sphere Books Limited
27 Wrights Lane, London W8 5TZ

First published in Great Britain by Jonathan Cape, 1986

Published by Sphere Books Ltd, 1987

TRADE
MARK

Set in Linotron Goudy
Printed and bound in Great Britain by
Cox & Wyman Ltd, Reading

TO TED

Chapter 1

Scheherazade Solomon began to wonder why her husband came home so late. One or two in the morning okay. But five or six? And sometimes not at all! Even if he was out playing pogo with the boys. Or was it bowling? She always got the two mixed up.

'After all,' she said to herself, 'After all, trains run all night to the Bronx. Even if he has to wait an hour or two for one.'

She had just begun to worry when she heard a fumbling at the lock. 'It couldn't be him so early,' she thought, 'it's only eleven o'clock.' She ran to the table where she had a gun hidden in case of burglars and went to the door. 'Who is it?' she called out.

'Me,' said Heathcliffe Solomon.

Holding the gun down at her side, Scheherazade opened the door with her left hand. There was Heathcliffe, looking dour and handsome, and holding something by his side too. An axe.

'What's that for?' asked Scheherazade, pointing.

Heathcliffe didn't say anything, he just looked at her, and advanced slowly.

'Don't be foolish,' said Scheherazade. 'I'll make you some tea.'

Heathcliffe snorted, which made him look like Laurence Olivier.

'Heathcliffe,' said Scheherazade calmly, 'what are you doing with that axe?'

'I am going to kill you.'

'You'll wake the neighbours.'

At this, Heathcliffe paused and Scheherazade seized the opportunity to ask, 'Why do you want to kill me, darling?'

'Because I cannot afford a divorce.'

'Why don't I make you a nice hot cup of tea first and then you can kill me?'

'Okay. But right after that.'

Scheherazade went into the kitchen.

Chapter 2

Heathcliffe sat slunched on the couch, his axe under his feet, while Scheherazade busied herself with the kettle. She slipped into an apron, a frothy little thing with a pocket for the gun. She put two Kleenexes on top of the gun to hide it. She thought of going out of the window but they lived on the nineteenth floor. Or of tiptoeing out of the apartment, but Heathcliffe would see her through the big mirror over the mantel and he could run faster than she.

She would use the gun only in self-defence. She didn't want to kill Heathcliffe; he was so good-looking. Why had he stopped loving her, she wondered? She was a marvellous cook, everybody said. And she was a good mother still to the children, who were grown up now. She snuck out of the kitchen into the bedroom and looked in the mirror. It was a long time since she had studied herself. 'Not so good,' she told herself honestly. 'But I'll give him some cake with his tea, then maybe he won't want to kill me.'

'There must be another woman,' she thought. 'That's what I get for letting him have a night a day out with the

boys. Maybe it isn't always the boys. It could be his secretary; I don't like that secretary, she looks snubbish to me. Perhaps I should be his secretary instead of playing the I Ching.*'*

So lost in thought was Scheherazade that she jumped when she heard Heathcliffe calling, 'Where's that tea? Hurry up or I'll kill you without it.'

Scheherazade hurried back into the kitchen and found that all the water had boiled away. She quickly refilled the kettle and poked her head into the living room. 'It's brewing,' she said. 'Wait for it, it will give you the strength.'

She returned to the bedroom and looked for the bottle of perfume she was saving for weddings and other important occasions. She closed her eyes and poured. Back in the kitchen, cutting the cake she had made that afternoon into six pieces, she filled a large teapot. 'If only I had a potion to put in here,' she thought. 'A love potion. But I don't.'

She was just about to make her entrance into the living room when she remembered her apron, gun and all. 'After all, the other woman wouldn't wear an apron,' she thought. 'That is the trouble with me, I'm too domesticated.'

She served Heathcliffe his tea and cake and asked nonchalantly, 'Guess who I met today?'

'How should I know?' answered Heathcliffe, reaching for more cake.

'Lord Crinkleton.'

'Who the hell is Lord Crinkleton?'

'You don't know who Lord Crinkleton is? I have spent many hours with Lord Crinkleton. I'll tell you about him sometime. A fascinating man.'

Heathcliffe looked at his wife suspiciously. He felt the axe under his feet. 'Tell me now.'

'To know who Lord Crinkleton is,' said Scheherazade, 'you have to really hear a lot about him because Lord Crinkleton is a very complicated character. After all,' and she looked Heathcliffe square in the eye, 'he is a lord.'

'So what?' said Heathcliffe uncomfortably.

'But I will begin,' said Scheherazade, 'and you can hear as much as you have time for.'

'You can begin,' said Heathcliffe, 'but you had better talk fast or you won't have time to end and that would be a shame. Unfinished stories are not artistic.'

'I will begin but I don't know how long it will take. People like Lord Crinkleton are not met with every day. Nor for that matter is Titsiepoo.'

'Who's Titsiepoo?'

'Titsiepoo is a staggering love of Lord Crinkleton with whom he happens to be very much involved.'

'You're putting me on. Nobody in this world is called Titsiepoo.'

'I swear to God there is a Titsiepoo. I'll swear on the Bible. Where is our Bible?'

'You gave it to our son-in-law to swear on and you know it.'

'Okay, then take my word for it. There is a Titsiepoo.'

Heathcliffe didn't say anything, he just looked at Scheherazade with his black eyes as if to say, 'Prove it.'

'To really tell you about Lord Crinkleton I should have to tell you about the way he met Titsiepoo. Yes, that is the way I shall begin.'

And Scheherazade Solomon began her story over their cup of tea.

Chapter 3

At three o'clock in the afternoon, Lord Crinkleton leaned back in his Rolls Royce. He was on his way to his job as Chairman of the Board.

'Chairman of the Board of what?' asked Heathcliffe.

'The Board of Directors. What else, silly?'

As Lord Crinkleton leaned back thinking of his activities that morning, a soft smile played about his lips. His activities had consisted mainly of making it in front of his polished five-dimensional mirror with a new chambermaid when she had brought him his breakfast. He thought of her with great relish.

After the chambermaid he had had to hurry so that he could get to his job that afternoon and he had hardly had time for lunch. 'Egad, I am a bit hungry,' he said to himself now, and took out a diamond-studded plastic case with a giant ruby in the centre in which he always kept a boiled potato. Tenderly he unwrapped it from its gold leaf casing.

'A boiled potato! Wasn't it cold?' asked Heathcliffe.

'He liked them cold,' said Scheherazade, 'or there would have been built-in thermostatic control.'

It was spring and a gentle breeze came through the window of the Rolls Royce, ruffling Lord Crinkleton's hair as he ate his boiled potato. His hair was dark and wavy over his handsome Greek-like brow and a great light of lewd intelligence shone from his aristocratic eyes. He was a tall man, you could see that even when he was leaning back, overshadowing other men by his very presence. The gentle breeze made Lord Crinkleton think very horny thoughts so that his organ swelled in his tailor-made trousers. These were of a banker's grey with a lot of extra material provided in that area. The tailor said he had never encountered an organ of such magnitude. 'They run in the family,' the lord had told him. 'However, mine is the largest on record. They seem to improve with each successive generation.'

Although Lord Crinkleton was proud of this gift of his, most of the time he thought nothing of it because it was with him all the time. However, he was constantly reminded that it was unusual by each new damsel who invariably would swoon at first sight of it. As a matter of fact, there were some damsels who swooned even after encountering it hundreds of times.

Once Lord Crinkleton had used his gift as a battering ram. A damsel with whom he had an assignation had been locked in her room by her husband, and was in dire distress at not being able to see the lord. Learning of her plight only when he arrived upon the scene, and hearing her piteous moans, the resourceful man did not waste time calling a locksmith or a safecracker. He merely took out his organ and pffft! the door gave way.

Of many such exploits is Lord Crinkleton the hero.

On this spring day Lord Crinkleton lit an eighteen-inch cigarette, specially made for him, with his gold lighter. He crossed his feet in his custom-made shoes and flicked a speck of dust that had had the nerve to alight on one of his sapphire cuff-links. He wriggled his left big toe in his twenty-five dollar pure silk socks, which reminded him of the manicurist who sometimes also gave him pedicures. He missed her; he hadn't seen her for almost a week. They were more than friends. Every time she came up to his penthouse on Park Avenue the manicure lasted four hours. At least.

Lord Crinkleton was thinking of having his bedroom redecorated, but in the meantime it would have to do. The bed was eight by eight so that nobody could fall off. It was a four-poster with shimmering curtains from India, transparent, embroidered in gold, silver and many other colours, and lavish with folds. The ceiling was made of bevelled mirrors so that you could watch yourself many times over and in various attitudes if you chose to look. On the walls were murals painted by world-famous artists. On one wall was Diana being caught by Apollo in the hunt. On another was Leda cavorting with the swan. Another wall was devoted to Indian sculpture from a love temple. The fourth had a large cubist painting of a very interesting couple getting to know each other. The fifth wall was covered with peacock feathers and sequins, while the sixth wall featured Aphrodite entertaining some of her gentlemen friends.

On the peacock wall was a beautiful sculpture of Lord Crinkleton's organ on which he hung his hat. The rugs were mostly skins: lion, tiger, leopard, polar bear, rare squirrel – things the lord had shot on hunting expeditions.

Every day Lord Crinkleton had new sheets put on his bed. In the summer they were satin, either midnight blue, ultra violet or Arabian tourmaline. In the winter he liked sable or mink.

When the lord had a guest in his bedroom marijuana fumes of the finest Acapulco Gold were wafted in through the air-conditioning system so that the couple would not have to bother smoking – they could just breathe. After the marijuana came perfume – Arpège. In one corner of the room was a fountain – wine specially selected by Lord Crinkleton's staff of tasters – and there were trees growing in tubs from which one could pick a fruit of the season: pomegranates, lichees, kumquats, mangoes, persimmons and kiwis.

Although Lord Crinkleton spent so much time in his bedroom this did not mean that he neglected his job as Chairman of the Board. Quite the contrary. His presence was necessary to run things.

'What kind of things?' asked Heathcliffe.

'The money. That gentleman ran the money. He was a very good Chairman of the Board.'

So here was our hero, on his way to Wall Street, with nothing on his mind but how to run the money and that it was time to see the manicurist again. He had finished his potato and was thinking about how good it was when he saw a line of men, three abreast, extending around the corner. More were running from every direction to join it. Lord Crinkleton pressed the inter-com button. 'Blaise,' he said to his chauffeur through the glass, 'what is that line of men, do you know? I don't see any movie house.'

'Shall I find out, sir?' asked Blaise.

'Please do.'

Blaise stopped, removed his driving gloves and put them in the glove compartment, which was packed with various things: his PhD degree in Philosophy, a few of the lord's old address books, a street guide, and a pair of the lord's silk pyjamas.

The pyjamas were for those times the lord got carried away and couldn't wait until he got home. On these occasions Lord Crinkleton pressed a button and presto! the window shades lowered, the back of the front seat dropped down and joined the back seat which moved forward and expanded, making the whole limousine a comfortable bed. Blaise would be told to go for a walk lasting at least two hours. Blaise did a lot of walking, but more often would find a place to stop off with one of his books. That is how he read for his doctorate.

Blaise got out of the car and started walking to the front of the line while Lord Crinkleton leaned back and pulled out another cigarette.

When Blaise returned he was very excited. 'It's Titsiepoo,' he said.

'I beg your pardon?'

'Titsiepoo. They're all waiting to buy their newspaper from Titsiepoo so that they can get an unobstructed view when their turn comes up.'

'Why? What's so special about her? Did you see her?'

'Not yet, I didn't want to keep you waiting, but I did speak to someone in the queue who said that she's America's Helen of Troy.'

'Really? Then why is she selling newspapers?'

'My lord,' Blaise pointed out, 'think what a volume of business she does. Besides, she has no overheads to speak of and she is her own boss. She sells magazines, too. Empires have been built by people who started as newspaper vendors. Sometimes they buy out the paper they are working for.'

'You have given me an idea. Perhaps we will buy out Titsiepoo. Bring her to me and we will have a look at her. And get me a *Times*.' Pressing a twenty-dollar bill into his chauffeur's hand, Lord Crinkleton leaned back in anticipation, an ecstatic leer on his handsome physiognomy.

In an hour Blaise came back. 'I finally got to see her. And while I waited I collected more details about her. That girl isn't going to leave her stand for twenty dollars . . . lots of guys hand her a twenty just to have the privilege of getting their paper out of her hand. She's only been here a week and she's already an institution. Sometimes the mayor sends her a private escort of a couple of cops so that she can get home in one piece.'

'Here's a hundred. No problem,' said Lord Crinkleton, opening his alligator wallet, fat with pictures of presidents and well-endowed damsels.

'I'll have to get in line again,' said Blaise, 'and I'm not sure that this is the way to do it.'

'Tell me about her.'

'I can't tell you.' Blaise's eyes went heavenward and he whispered reverently, 'You have to see for yourself.'

'I shall,' said his employer, and to Blaise's amazement, he got out of the car.

So elegant did the lord look that the crowd made way for him and in no time at all he reached the head of the line.

Titsiepoo was sitting in her newspaper stand, which was hung with magazine cover girls who looked vapid and anaemic next to herself. All kinds of hootsy-tootsies were displaying their charms. Titsiepoo did not need to take her clothes off to display hers. They were just there.

When Lord Crinkleton clapped his elegant eyes upon her, he could not take another step forward for fear of splintering her news stand with his yardstick.

Titsiepoo was 52, 19, 38. But measurements cannot adequately tell the story. So voluptuous were Titsiepoo's endowments, so upright and outstanding, that the ordinary observer would have expected her to topple over. Lord Crinkleton, experienced man that he was, briefly wondered about this himself. But at the sight of the lord, Titsiepoo, as if drawn by invisible wires, stood up, and he could see that the lovely lass had the perfect balance for her upper half: two lovely orbs to sit upon.

The girl's golden hair, flaming like the sun, fell in waves to the middle of her back. She had a face that nobody can describe, not even I, because who can describe an angel? Especially an angel with blue eyes and soccer balls. Titsiepoo was all peaches and cream and, as he gazed at her ardently, Lord Crinkleton decided that such a jewel should not be left to the pack of wolves lined up in front of her stand for several blocks, even though there appeared to be a few other board directors and assorted gentlemen of

that ilk lying in wait. She was much too good for them and should be kept only for him. He would decorate this beauty with emeralds and diamonds and put her in a velvet room befitting such a creature.

'And that,' said Scheherazade, 'is how Lord Crinkleton met Titsiepoo. That is how the whole thing came about, very casually, out of nowhere, when neither of them in the least expected it; that is how this important meeting occurred that was to figure prominently in both their lives. That is how the great Lord Crinkleton, the pride of his tailor, the joy of so many damsels, one of the best chairmen of the board, met the supernaturally endowed Titsiepoo, whose fame and glory will go down in the history of America. Titsiepoo and Lord Crinkleton!'

'So what happened?' asked Heathcliffe. 'You're killing me with suspense.'

'No,' Scheherazade reminded him, 'it is you who are doing the killing.'

'Well', said Heathcliffe sheepishly, 'I'm a little tired now. Suppose I do it tomorrow night after you finish the story?'

'Tomorrow night I'll change his mind,' thought Scheherazade.

Chapter 4

The next morning Heathcliffe got up early, removed Scheherazade's keys from her purse, and had the phone disconnected. Then he woke her and told her what he had done.

'But who's running away?' she asked.

'And just so you don't get any ideas about hollering for help from the window or calling out to anyone who rings the doorbell, I've locked up all your clothes except for the ones you keep in my closet.'

'But those are out of style and you know it! I can't let anybody see me in those, not even the newspaper boy.'

A happy smile lit Heathcliffe's face. 'I know.'

'But I have to get out to do the shopping.'

'I'll do it.' Heathcliffe put his axe in his attaché case, flung Scheherazade a glowering glance, and was gone.

'If only he would divorce me,' Scheherazade thought, 'we could live in sin. That would be nice.' She smiled as she remembered running around the moors of Washington Heights, gathering weeds with Heathcliffe before they were married.

Prompted by such thoughts, she made her way to the bedroom, and once again faced herself in the full-length mirror. She spent the rest of the morning doing push-ups.

Oh, she would have to turn her whole life around, go back to being the girl she had been on the white cliffs of Washington Heights, a wild, free creature unburdened by thoughts of what to make for dinner.

'Dinner!' she thought. It had been so long since Heathcliffe had been home for one. Would he be dining with the Other Woman tonight or would he hurry home to hear her story? She would make him a pot roast and potato pancakes, just in case he showed up, and a lemon pie, his favourite dessert.

She spent the next hour painting her toe nails, then did the cooking, after which she went to his closet and looked over her old clothes. None of them would do. Then she remembered a negligée that she hadn't worn since before the babies. Eagerly she dug deep into a drawer and tried it on. It didn't meet in the middle any more, but so what? She would sew a piece of ribbon along the edge. And tomorrow she would do some more push-ups. Maybe she would even do some yoga. Her life was in Titsiepoo's hands. And Lord Crinkleton's. So she thought of them for several hours, until she heard the key turn in the lock and Heathcliffe, the light of her life, attaché case in one hand, and a bag of groceries in the other, walked in.

'For me?' asked Scheherazade, as if he had presented her with roses.

'I didn't know if you had enough food in the house for your last meal.'

'It just so happens I made you a lovely dinner – pot roast and potato pancakes – but you can eat these things tomorrow,' said Scheherazade cheerfully.

'I ate, but I will have a small portion. I cannot resist potato pancakes so I may as well have some pot roast to go with them.'

Noting to herself that it was a long time since her husband had had dinner with her, Scheherazade set the table in silence. Heathcliffe looked a little surprised at her outfit, but said nothing.

'And,' said Scheherazade, 'for when I continue my story, right after dinner, I have baked you a lemon pie entirely by hand. I did not use my Mixmaster.'

'Start the story now,' said Heathcliffe, 'while we eat. I

came home early so you'd have time to finish it tonight.'

'While we're having tea, if you don't mind, so I can concentrate and serve you properly. In the meantime, eat your potato pancakes.'

Chapter 5

As Lord Crinkleton clapped eyes on Titsiepoo, Titsiepoo, naturally, clapped eyes on him. Such mutual clappings are not rare in our society but it is not often that both parties are so pleased as were these two. Titsiepoo's blue eyes blazed with a heavenly ardour as her glance took in the lord's noble profile and proportions, which were further enhanced by the quite apparent presence of his yardstick.

'I'll have a *Times*,' said the lord, who had decided that it would be vulgar to hand her a paltry hundred-dollar bill, and gave her thirty cents instead. As he pressed it into her tiny hand, however, he said very softly, 'I have my car here if you'd care to go for a little drive in the country.'

'Call for me after work,' said Titsiepoo. 'I'll be through at six.' She would have preferred to go with him there and then but she could not let anything interfere with her career.

'It is such a beautiful day, wouldn't you like to go

now?' asked Lord Crinkleton, who really didn't give a hoot about the beautiful day.

'I'm not dressed for the country,' she replied, with a stunning sweep of her upper storey.

'Then we can either stay in the city or I can rustle you up a little outfit.'

'Either one,' said Titsiepoo.

Lord Crinkleton leapt back to his car. 'Gad, Blaise, why didn't you tell me, man? We wasted five minutes with your vague implications. It's three thirty already and we have to hurry to my furrier's to have an outfit made by six.'

Blaise ran back for Titsiepoo's measurements, then sped down the street while Lord Crinkleton thought. If they remained in the city she might want to go to work the next day or something silly like that. He was both intrigued and perplexed. But on vivid reflection he decided that she was well worth waiting for and asked Blaise whether he thought sable or leopard would most become her.

"Definitely leopard. She's a bit of a wild one.'

'Ah, yes, to start with anyway,' said the lord.

He continued with his thoughts. He would make his appearance at the Board as soon as he had put in his order for Titsiepoo's outfit. Blaise could wait at the furrier's to see that the instructions were carried out faithfully; he knew about such matters. It also helped that he had seen the wearer and could reassure the furrier that the measurements given were, indeed, correct. Dreamily the lord wondered where this angel could possibly buy her clothes ready made. Perhaps she ran them up herself. What a lot of material a dress must take, he thought approvingly. Good for the national economy.

It was now four thirty-five and the Board meeting always ended at five, but Lord Crinkleton decided to show up anyway because he had nowhere else to go until Blaise called for him. Of course this would have given him enough time for three or four quickies with his secretary but, since he might stay at his lodge for several days, he decided on the former course of action as the wisest.

He reached the board room at a quarter to five, just as the members were thinking of going home, but even so they seemed genuinely glad to see him. After all the usual greetings the lord called the meeting to order and the items of business came up. The first was for the lord to decide how to get the troops out of South America.

'That is easy,' said Lord Crinkleton. 'We get them out by getting them in deeper so that they come out the other end. Anybody knows that. Or send them to Russia instead.'

There were enthusiastic exclamations of 'Praise be the lord!' and a telegram was immediately dispatched to the President. Lord Crinkleton made decisions very quickly; there was none of the shilly-shallying that goes on at other board meetings throughout our mighty land.

The next item on the agenda was a food package. A woman had written in from Albany, the capital of the State, that she couldn't open her package of frozen strawberries. This was really a more pressing matter than getting the troops out, but the Board knew that the lord always liked to serve his country first, putting it above his private interests.

'Here is the package,' said the president of the company. 'We were wondering what to do because it was produced by a top firm of industrial designers. If the letter were from anywhere but Albany I would say that the woman can't read instructions.'

'Has any of you gentlemen tried opening the package?' asked the Chairman of the Board.

There was a gasp and then everyone exchanged glances. The lord had done it again! The president called for a bowl to be brought; a secretary was sent down to buy one, for it was discovered that none existed in the organization; and the package problem was tabled till the next meeting so as not to keep the lord waiting. Within fifteen minutes he had taken care of everything and adjourned the meeting on time. As usual.

Lord Crinkleton strode into his private office, past Nancy, his secretary, sitting at her rosewood desk. He had begun to wonder whether he should warm up for Titsiepoo by having a quick one with Nancy, when Blaise radioed up that it was time for them to go.

'Good-bye, my lovely,' said the lord, a vague suggestion of promise in his voice. 'I may be out of town for a few days, in which case I shall communicate with you from time to time.'

'Good night, my lord,' said Nancy. What had she to look forward to until his return? She reminded herself that they also serve who only sit and wait.

Heathcliffe had been sitting and waiting all this time for Scheherazade to serve him the pie. He had finished with tea long ago. Quietly, he reminded her.

Scheherazade fetched the pie; she had quite forgotten it in the enthusiasm of her tale. Then she continued.

Lord Crinkleton opened the box containing Titsiepoo's present. It was a lovely little leopard suit: a demi-bra, slinky trousers with a piece of tail, and a form-fitting cap with leopard ears.

How wonderful that he could entrust Blaise with such important commissions. What if the fellow ever left him and went off to be a philosophy professor or some such thing? He shuddered. 'Not likely,' thought the lord. 'I pay him more.'

Despite the fact that there were still hundreds of

customers, Titsiepoo was just closing her stand. These men, who ordinarily left their offices at a quarter to five to beat the rush, would be missing their commuter trains. They were now cheerfully thinking up excuses to give their wives for being late for dinner again that week. Students were skipping their classes, dates were being stood up on street corners. It could have rained, it could have hailed, but nothing could have stayed these men and boys from their appointed round. Every time Titsiepoo raised her arms, projecting her already impossible-to-ignore charms; every time she moved her ass, a happy sigh rose from the crowd. People who in ten years would never dare talk to each other now exchanged observations. She was a great democratizing force in the city, and to think that she had been in business only one week, had only just begun her good works. Imagine how it would be when she had been there a month!

Just then Lord Crinkleton's fifteen-foot car came gliding up and Blaise jumped out to collect Titsiepoo. She and Blaise exchanged hot looks in spite of the fact that Blaise had been trained in yoga. As he opened the door of the car, Titsiepoo toppled neatly into the lord's waiting arms. Fiercely, Lord Crinkleton clasped her to his macho chest, mingling his American nose with her flower of a face. 'Town or country?' asked Blaise.

'Would you like a little drive in the country, my dear?' the lord asked Titsiepoo. 'We can stop off at my lodge where I keep a fire blazing all winter just for the hell of it.'

'I love the country,' replied Titsiepoo, 'but I cannot be home too late because I have to get ready for my job in the morning.'

'Don't worry,' said the lord, who actually had other plans. 'We shall get you back whenever you so desire.'

They were now outside the city limits. Blaise veered off the road into the lord's private lane hidden behind some bushes which moved aside at the touch of a button located in a tree. No one else knew about this lane except a few mooses, partridges, and other such who sometimes used it as a short cut when they had to rush home. 'We could have taken the helicopter, my dear,' he breathed into Titsiepoo's little ear, 'but you would not have seen much of the landscape, so I believe it is better this way.'

Titsiepoo, who had seen almost nothing thus far, thought she ought to take a look at the landscape. Accordingly, she pressed her nose to the glass. A full round moon rode the sky.

'And that,' said Scheherazade, 'is where the curtain drops on this act of Titsiepoo and Lord Crinkleton because I have to get to bed.'

'Did he wait till he got to the lodge at least until he . . .?' asked Heathcliffe.

'I will tell you tomorrow night.'

Chapter 6

Heathcliffe left the house before Scheherazade awoke next morning. She made herself a cup of coffee, did her push-ups, took a quick look in the mirror, and decided to spend some time inventing a new hairdo for herself instead of baking a pie. 'New regime,' she told herself. 'Titsiepoo wouldn't bake pies.'

That evening Heathcliffe came home in time for dinner, which he wolfed down so Scheherazade could continue her story. Scheherazade, again in her negligée, hair flowing to her shoulders as she hadn't worn it in years, settled herself on the couch, legs curled up at her side, and began.

Yes, Lord Crinkleton waited until he got to the lodge. This was not his usual practice. Normally Blaise would go walking in the woods where he would build himself a little bonfire to read for his degree in Neurotics. But this time Lord Crinkleton decided to wait because there was so much of Titsiepoo to enjoy.

The lodge was not as palatial as the lord's town

apartment. It was more of a fun place, used for knocking around. Instead of bevelled mirrors and murals some of the walls were papered with the currency of different countries – dollars, yen, Deutschemarks, whatever was in fashion at the moment – and all of the rooms had fireplaces. Several heads were mounted in the hall of the lord's den: an elk, a water buffalo, and those of two rival board members.

Off the living room was a bar that could have been a small liquor store. The fact is that the lord could drink anyone under the table. There were those who facetiously called him 'Lord Drinkleton', just as at his office he was reverently referred to as 'Lord Thinkleton', and at the furrier's, 'Lord Minkleton'.

On the other side of the living room was the smoking room for those who did not drink or for those who did both. Here the lord kept his marijuana from all over the world, including the most orgasmic strains of Manhattan Flower Pot Grey. And bhang from India, made into puddings for those who did not enjoy smoking but wished to imbibe the delicious effects of Indian lore.

Leading off from the smoker was the games room with a billiard table, dozens of games, a one-ton weight for the lord to lift, and the dog, Emerson, who preferred the games room to all of the other chambers, so his house was installed there. Emerson was large and brown with purple spots. Nobody knew what breed, if any, but his master didn't care for he loved this animal who had followed him home one day as he was striding across the fields. Naturally there were games outside, too, such as archery, croquet, riding horses and a swing.

Emerson took an immediate liking to Titsiepoo and followed her around. Titsiepoo thought it might be because of the way she fell out of her dress when she bent to pat him, but the lord did not think so. 'He has his own interests,' he said, 'which he finds at the next lodge several miles away. Otherwise, he's really quite an introvert. Likes plays on television if they're worthwhile.'

Titsiepoo's ears pricked up at this because she dearly loved intellectuals, especially if they were males. 'What else does he do?' she asked, very interested.

'Just about everything but read.'

So impressed was Titsiepoo by this wonderful dog that she patted him again, with the same result as before at her neckline. This time she was embarrassed, thinking that an intellectual dog like Emerson would think her immodest. She need not have worried; the admiration was mutual.

Meanwhile, Lord Crinkleton stood in speechless awe. Although he had done some initial exploring of her celestial globes in the car, the moon had not lit them as well as the room did. 'What a privileged man am I!' he thought happily at the sight of the pink roses that bloomed upon these hillocks of passion.

'I'm a little hungry,' said Titsiepoo, by now completely back in her dress.

'The footman has prepared us a repast for whenever you are ready, my dear. But I thought you might like me to show you the rest of the lodge first. You haven't seen the upstairs yet,' suggested her host, pointedly.

'I'd like dinner if you don't mind. I haven't eaten since noon.'

'Of course,' said the lord, who was quite unaccustomed to these kinds of priorities. 'Perhaps you'd like to change into this little country outfit I bought you.'

'How thoughtful!' exclaimed Titsiepoo. 'I'll go and slip it on.'

'I'll have the footman show you to your dressing room. And I'll do a quick change myself.' The lord had to change. Something had just happened to his trousers.

'For crying out loud,' spluttered Heathcliffe. 'He's taking too long. I would have shown her the upstairs already. At this rate the story will take forever.'

'This very slowness of Titsiepoo, this insistence upon eating, which she hadn't done for eight hours, is one of the things that intrigued Lord Crinkleton about her. Titsiepoo had more than physical beauty; she had fine sensibilities. Now if you want I can skip over part of the story, but then you won't know the psychology of the characters which is so important in understanding how future developments come to pass. I can do whatever you want me to, Heathcliffe,' said Scheherazade, careful to keep the longing from her voice.

'Go on with the story,' said Heathcliffe gruffly. 'Only hurry up.'

'Yes, of course.'

Lord Crinkleton showered and changed into dark trousers with a red velveteen jacket and a white ruffled shirt, for he never dressed formally at the lodge. He put on his new watch which, the ad said, was the latest seduction weapon. Of course, Lord Crinkleton had his own built-in weapon but he wore the watch anyway. He sprinkled himself with his special blend of cologne and went downstairs to wait for Titsiepoo.

He had had his boiled potato rather late, and would have preferred to do other things, but he did not want Titsiepoo to be hungry. How liberally nature had endowed that girl! He said a little prayer of thanks.

During the lord's prayer Titsiepoo bounced down the stairs, looking enchanting in her new outfit although the demi-bra fell just short of exhibiting her all, due to a mathematical miscalculation on the great man's part. However, he had memory to sustain him. The lord did not know where to look first because, for some reason, which he was at a loss to explain, he was also drawn to her angelic face.

'Shall I make you a drink, my dear?' he asked, regretting that he had to succumb to this formality, but not wishing to appear in the rush that he was. The sooner she ate the sooner he could show this naïve girl his wonderful upstairs where things would happen that would make her forget all about going to work and her career. 'Or would you like to eat right away?' He took a step towards the dining room.

'Let's have a drink first.' Titsiepoo snuggled into a chair before the fire.

Silently, the lord gnashed his teeth a little, but went about making the girl a wicked brew which would have knocked her out if she weren't going to eat immediately afterwards. He rang for the butler to bring some canapés, including some devilish eggs of which he was particularly fond.

As Titsiepoo sat sipping her drink and looking into the fire she threw the lord an angelic smile just as he was popping one of his devilish eggs into his mouth. He smiled back wolfily, happy that she would soon be finished with her damned drink. Finally, giving her his arm, he led her into the dining room, which was Roman-style with couches. Thus ensconced, it did not matter that Lord Crinkleton had miscalculated on the cut of Titsiepoo's demi-bra; it might as well not have been there. She, however, did not notice this, as she was observing how the lord used his yardstick rather than his elbow with which to prop himself up.

While the fountain in the centre of the room failed to dampen the enthusiasms of Venus and Apollo, a Hungarian musician fiddled one of Nero's compositions, drowning out the soft pad of the footman as he went back and forth with trays loaded with gastronomical achievements.

Titsiepoo ate daintily while the lord licked her fingers and smacked his lips. 'Aren't you eating?' asked Titsiepoo.

'Ah, my dear, I cannot think of food in such company.' Light as a butterfly, his hand rested momentarily on a hemisphere, thence flitted to her tiny waist which served as a mere stem for what blossomed above. 'Such a frail little thing!' thought Lord Crinkleton. 'I wonder if she gets enough to eat?'

Meanwhile Titsiepoo was on her third dessert. She

did not always eat like a raven, but there were a number of new things to be tasted. After a demi-tasse in which the lord joined her because he could down it with one pinkie, Titsiepoo declared that she had finished dining. 'Now show me the rest of your domicile.'

Had the lord been a lesser man he would have thrown his hat into the air, but he seldom wore one indoors. Nor did he wish to appear too eager; let her be the one who had to wait for him even though he was bursting with desire. So hot was Lord Crinkleton after gazing at Titsiepoo's little body encased in its leopard-skin shell that he 'remembered' an errand he had to perform and excused himself for a few minutes. He ran out into the cold air without his coat, warmed by the fire that blazed within him. Entering the stable door he called out, 'Dorothy!' but there was no answer from the livery girl. 'She must be in her room,' thought the lord, but he had no intention of going

there, as it was at least forty feet away, so he did one of the horses, a sorrel, the honour. She was his favourite although he liked them all. Lord Crinkleton had won well-deserved fame not only as a ladies' man but also as a horseman.

Galloping back to the lodge, the lord appeared before Titsiepoo, advising her that he had had to look after one of the horses. 'But she's fine now,' he added. 'Has anything of interest happened during my absence, my dear?' He had been gone only five minutes.

'No, nothing momentous. I've been thinking.'

'Thinking!' The lord was astonished. 'Why have you been doing that?' Then, out of his great interest in things, he asked. 'What have you been thinking *about*?'

'I was thinking about my life.'

So unaccustomed was the lord to the idea that women had thoughts, particularly a woman to whom the gods had been so generous, that he stopped in his tracks. 'Tell me about it, my dear.'

'I think I'll kill you now,' said Heathcliffe.

'If you want. But why now? I can't get away and you can do it any time.'

'Because. I'm tired and it was time for them to go upstairs. And that's where I have to go now, to bed, and I haven't heard the climax of this loony story yet. I am frustrated and you're going to die.'

'Okay, Heathcliffe. You may as well get it over with.'

'But then I won't know what happened.'

Scheherazade shrugged her shoulders.

'All right. You can have until tomorrow night, but that's all. That story better be finished by then or you will be.'

'See you tomorrow night.'

Chapter 7

The next evening, Scheherazade continued.

'My earliest years were ordinary enough,' said Titsiepoo. 'I used to sit in our garden and watch the flowers come up. I even became a Girl Scout.' The lord looked at her admiringly.

'In the summer we went to the seashore where I met the same friends every year and we played in the sun and the sand. I suppose I was happy because I can't remember being sad.'

'Who would have thought,' mused Lord Crinkleton, 'that this beauteous creature would turn out to be so intelligent? How well she expresses herself! What turns of phrase! What nobility of mind!' He was quite overcome with his discovery and, to his surprise, inflamed by it. 'Be right back, my dear,' he said to Titsiepoo. 'I have to check on the horse.'

But Lord Crinkleton did not go to the stable. Once a day was enough for that horse. Running again without his coat, he moved a branch of a tree to the right and a small pink marble vault opened up at his feet. From it he took his motorcycle, a shoulder-length wig and a guitar. Placing the wig on his head and the guitar under his arm, the lord zoomed off to a rock concert a few miles away. He hung outside the hall no more than forty seconds when he was approached by a groupie who took him by the yardstick and led him to her tent. It was dark, he could hardly see her face, but she felt nice. 'Sorry I have to dash off like this, Baby,' he said. 'I'll be back sometime soon and we'll dig each other again and I can give you my autograph. In the meantime here's some acid I just copped.'

Zapping back to the hunting lodge in a mere matter of minutes, not even out of breath, he was ready to listen to Titsiepoo's bell-like voice again with perfect calm and equanimity.

'How is the horse?' she asked.

'Seems fine. Maybe I'll look in on her again one more time, and after that I should be all right.'

'In school I was just like everybody else,' Titsiepoo continued. 'I got "A's" in those subjects I really liked and "C" when I found them a bore.

'One evening I heard my father say to my mother, "I hope our little daughter will grow up to be a great beauty."

'"Do not wish it on her!" cried my mother, who had been busy staving off the men at the seashore till my father arrived for his two weeks' vacation. "Too much beauty can be a curse."

'But my father paid no attention and, determined

that my looks should feed his ego, did a little research. Unbeknownst to my mother, he took me to a lady who claimed that she had studied magic and could perform miracles. "I'm sure she will not turn her into a toad," my father laughed to himself, and paid her handsomely. Accordingly, I was given a magic potion.

'Next day I became as you now see me. My mother was aghast. My father was beside himself. He had not expected anything so drastic. As for me, I thought my new body very comfortable. I could sit on the floor without needing a pillow, and couldn't believe that it was mine. My father took me back to the witch, but she had just been jailed for reading a Communist book on dialectical materialism. We went to see her but she pleaded the Fifth Amendment. Besides, she said I looked very nice and that most young women would give their eye teeth to look like me. I was only fourteen at the time and it was hard to think of myself as a young woman.

'In school next day all the boys' desks levitated. I did not know why or that it had anything to do with me because I was just sitting there as I always had. However, when riots occurred in the halls with boys from all over the school wanting to get a look at me or brush up against me, the principal got wind of it. Once he had seen me, he sent for my father and suggested that I be removed from the school or he would not be responsible for anything that might happen.

'This made my father over-cautious. He investigated private schools and found that most of the girls' schools had some male teachers so he decided that I should be tutored at home.'

'Excuse me,' said Lord Crinkleton, 'but I don't like the way Emerson is looking at you.'

'Oh, we were talking before when you were out tending to the horse. We're just friends, that's all. We've established communion.'

'I never saw him look at anybody like that before. I think I'll put him in his dog house.'

'Oh, please leave him here, Crinky. I like him.'

Flattered that she addressed him so affectionately, the lord assented. 'Go on, my dear, with your raconteur. I'm sorry I interrupted.'

'Why should he be jealous of a dog?' asked Heathcliffe.

'Because Emerson was looking at Titsiepoo's protuberances. I have told you that he was a very intellectual dog and he could see that this was a very superior woman. He was impressed that she could talk, and he was listening to the story too. Enraptured, like the lord.'

'My father hired two eunuchs to tutor me, and they taught me everything I know.'

'Eunuchs! They know so little of the world. What could they teach you?'

'Mostly about sex.'

Involuntarily, the lord leered forward.

'And other things, too, of course, but they liked to talk about sex because they weren't practising it. And they told me that men are interested in women for just ONE THING.'

'I don't know what that could be,' muttered the nobleman.

'So I determined that there would be more to me than ONE THING.'

'There is,' came the nod.

'I decided that I would develop myself.'

'But you did, my dear.'

'Be serious!' Titsiepoo spoke sharply to the lord, which no one, man or woman, had ever done. Surprised, he kept quiet for a few minutes.

'I decided that I wanted to do something important with my life. Like teach kindergarten. Or become a curator in an art museum. I haven't decided which yet. In the meantime, as soon as I became eighteen I ran away from home, which was last week. I shall work until I have enough money for college. And that brings us up to the present.'

'Have there been many men in your life, my dear?'

'I was pretty well kept under lock and key by my parents, so that there hasn't been much chance until this week. Opportunities have been countless.

However, I have a feeling that all of these men are only interested in ONE THING.'

'How do you know that I am not interested in only ONE THING, too, my dear?' asked the lord, who was an honourable man.

'Perhaps you are,' said Titsiepoo. 'But I, too, ever since having been taught by my tutors, am interested in ONE THING.'

Fiercely, Lord Crinkleton clasped the lovely Titsiepoo to him and vaulted to the top of the stairs that led to the bedroom.

Scheherazade yawned.

'If you tell me you're sleepy now, I swear I'll kill you.'

'I will tell you no such thing,' said Scheherazade, only she collapsed into slumber on the couch. Heathcliffe shook her; she opened her eyes and dropped off again.

Tomorrow he'd have to do it. He'd get rid of her for sure.

Chapter 8

Scheherazade remembered something. The gun. The gun was still in her apron pocket which was locked in the closet with the rest of her clothing. Of course, if she could get into the closet she would have access to all of her clothes and be able to call for help out of the window. That would be too bad because she really didn't want to kill Heathcliffe or to call for help. She wanted Heathcliffe to love her.

What she needed was a leopard suit, but she would have to settle for making herself something out of the bedspread. A sari. That was it; tonight she'd be an Indian. She would make a curry too, to go with it.

Maybe there was something more drastic than push-ups. They didn't seem to be that effective; besides, they made her so tired that she had to take a nap which would put back the weight she had lost.

She finished the sari. She finished cooking, as well as her elaborate ablutions. When Heathcliffe wasn't home by eight she decided to have dinner alone. She remembered how he used to come racing home to her at lunch hour *without taking time out to eat. Where was he now at the most exciting part of her story?*

At eleven o'clock the key turned. It was Heathcliffe, complete with axe. 'I've eaten,' he said, his eyes taking in her new costume and, she thought, not displeased, 'so we can finish the story.'

'Of course, my dear.'

As I have already reconnoitred, Lord Crinkleton reached the upstairs landing with one jump of his vaulting pole, the precious Titsiepoo in his arms. There they were, alone at last. Seating her on his pole for a minute while he lit a cigarette, the lord gazed long and ardently into the eyes of the lovely creature. Their lips met, their arms entwined. Carefully, so as not to disturb her, the lord walked over to the huge bed and parted the ostrich-feather curtains. The blankets were folded back in readiness, the pillow cases were hand-embroidered with a 'C', strobe lights played about, diamonds glistened like dewdrops on the curtains. In one swift motion the lord undid the cleverly concealed snap-out crotch thoughtfully provided in the leopard-skin pants while with the other hand he cast aside the top. Titsiepoo took off her hat. And then . . . their love was consumed!

Much later, they were interrupted by a cock crowing outside the window. 'Thank you, my dear,' said the lord, who never stopped being a gentleman, and removed his suit, which he hadn't yet had time to do.

'Thank you!' said Titsiepoo, clutching his toe just in case he was thinking of jumping out of bed.

But she did not yet know the lord. 'I should like to be able to thank you again,' he said.

Titsiepoo closed her angelic eyes and let the lord do with her as he would. 'Thank you,' he said again, after a couple of hours.

'Thank *you*,' said Titsiepoo, for this girl had been very well brought up, remember, with eunuchs and everything. As a matter of fact, the next time she said 'Thank you' first.

'Thank you, thank you, thank you!' answered her lover, carried away in the heat of the moment, waving his pole aloft. And, seeing it again available, the lovely creature took full possession of it.

'Thank you!' screamed the lord after a time, lying there and watching the steam rise.

'Don't mention it,' said Titsiepoo.

'Tell me, my dear,' Lord Crinkleton asked, 'for I am

curious about something. You said that there had been no men in your life and yet I do not seem to have been the first. Unless, as is the case with so many damsels, you have gone horseback riding perhaps?'

'No,' answered Titsiepoo truthfully. 'I have not gone horseback riding. And, as I have informed you, my teachers taught me all the facts of life. Being kept under lock and key, however, I had no opportunity to conduct any experiments to find out for myself whether what they told me would prove to be as agreeable in my case as they claimed. In short, I was curious. One day, reading in the *Wall Street Journal* about the banana craze, that there had been a big increase in sales because young people were smoking them, it gave me an idea. So I went to the kitchen and got some bananas. Only I didn't smoke them.'

'That was clever,' said the lord approvingly.

'Was it?' asked Titsiepoo. 'I think I prefer the real thing.'

'Then you shall have it, my dear,' said Lord Crinkleton.

When they had duly thanked each other, Titsiepoo sat up with a start. 'My God! What time is it, Crinky?'

'Why, my dear? We have all day.'

'I have to go to my job.'

'Forget about the job for today.'

'Crinky, I am a newspaperwoman. Newspaperwomen can't forget about their jobs. The newspaper must get sold just as the show must go on.'

'Scheherazade,' said Heathcliffe. 'I should like to be

able to thank you. Let's go to bed. You'll tell me about her career tomorrow night.'

'Thank you,' said Scheherazade.

Chapter 9

Heathcliffe Solomon was not a bad man; he just had a problem. Tiptoeing past the sleeping Scheherazade the next morning, he left a glass of orange juice by the bed, for that is what she liked the minute she opened her eyes. 'I wish I didn't have to do it,' he muttered aloud, 'I really wish I didn't. But I can give her another night or two. After all, she was a good wife to me. Sometimes a wonderful wife.'

He would have to be firm. Gentle but firm, he thought, gripping his attaché case.

In the meantime Scheherazade was having a dream. The dream was about Titsiepoo and Blaise. 'But,' she told herself when she awoke and had had her orange juice which she was so pleased to find that the tears gushed forth, 'I won't tell him about Blaise just yet. Blaise will come a little later. That is, if I'm still around.'

However, she did not keep this promise to herself.

An idea of monstrous implications had found its way into the indefatigable mind of Lord Crinkleton. 'Begone, wretch,' said the lord to the monstrous idea.

But it kept on coming back. The idea was that he should marry Titsiepoo.

'That would be an impossibility,' the lord told himself. 'Marriage means fidelity and I do not have time for that sort of thing. I am too busy making bevies of beauties happy. How they would miss me! Of course there are a few of them I would miss, too, but the country would absolutely fall apart with hosts of damsels unable either to go to work or to cook dinner. The nation would become undernourished, not to mention the fall in production. And this would happen not only in our great democracy but also wherever in the world I set foot. Nay, it is not feasible that I create yet another deprived segment of the population.

'What I shall do with my little darling,' decided this miraculous man, 'is put her where I can keep an eye on her at least some of the time. In one of my apartments perhaps.'

So instead of a ring he presented his sweetheart with a box from Tartier's which contained the Hope Diamond in the centre of a magnificent emerald necklace. 'How beautiful!' exclaimed the delighted girl. 'I shall accept this present because it is small and I shall wear it to work tomorrow. I don't want ever to take it off.'

The lord smiled indulgently, pleased at her freshness and naïveté. A spoiled girl would start a whole collection of necklaces whereas Titsiepoo never wanted to take this one off. She continued to astonish him with her qualities.

After dinner in the Roman dining room, during

which Emerson came in to sit in front of his new mistress, the couple decided to cavort in the fountain. Reluctantly, Titsiepoo removed her necklace because she did not want it to get wet. Seeing them thus occupied, Emerson made off with the necklace. Its disappearance was not noted till the couple had come out of the fountain whereupon Lord Crinkleton immediately suspected Emerson. 'Emerson, you cur!' he exclaimed harshly. 'What have you done with that necklace?' Emerson looked at him reproachfully for speaking to him like that. In vain the lord searched his sterling silver dog house and the games room; the jewels were nowhere to be found. 'He's hidden it, the scamp,' said the lord. 'I don't understand, he's never done anything like this before. But it will turn up, it has to be somewhere in the lodge.'

'Let's look for it now,' said Titsiepoo, disturbed at the loss of so beautiful a thing.

'Later,' said Lord Crinkleton, suddenly getting the impulse to stroke her little ears with his magic wand. Reluctantly, the lovely creature turned her attention from the emerald necklace back to the irresistible lord. And so they spent the night paying tribute to each other, finally falling asleep at ten o'clock the next morning. They did not awaken until dinner time and Titsiepoo missed her job again. 'Oh dear,' she moaned, 'what will my customers do? They'll think I'm out of business.'

'They'll get some work done,' said the lord. 'Think of all the man hours that are lost waiting for your papers.'

But Titsie did not hear him. Her desire was to serve her customers, further her career as a newspaper-woman, and commence her studies for the higher things she planned.

The two new lovers were awakened early the next afternoon by a call from Nancy, who asked the lord if he could come to the office for a while to make decisions.

Lord Crinkleton summoned Blaise but was told that the chauffeur had gone to a quiet spot in the woods where he was writing another doctoral dissertation on the role of the comma in the writings of James Joyce and its effect on the mental health of Samuel Beckett, and that it would take about twenty minutes to fetch him. 'Never mind,' said the lord, 'I'll fly the helicopter myself.' And so he did, first collecting his boiled potato from the footman and telling the golden one to amuse herself during his absence of a few hours.

On his arrival Lord Crinkleton was informed that he had been invited to China to a ping-pong tournament and the president wanted to know whether to accept for him.

'Certainly. Tell my secretary exactly when so she can remind me and find out which side they want me to play on.'

This done, the president brought up a question that had been bothering some members of the board. 'My lord,' he asked, 'what is the sound of one hand clapping?'

'We have put in a hard day, gentlemen,' said Lord Crinkleton, his lips smiling engagingly, 'especially with the strawberry problem which we shall be working on. So I move we adjourn the meeting until further notice.'

The meeting was adjourned forthwith and the lord went in to see the desperate Nancy whom he found furiously riding her rocking horse. Of course he couldn't stay too long because someone very dear was waiting for him at the lodge. However, he was truly fond of Nancy, so he gave her a quickie after she pointed out that she had had his couch redone during his absence. 'Ah, yes,' he said, 'we must try it out. Why should we always stand here behind the filing cabinet?'

'Because the springs were broken,' Nancy reminded him.

'My compliments to the upholsterer,' said the Chairman of the Board. He was about to don his hat when the fine secretary suggested that he might wish to look at the medals and other honours that had come for him during his brief absence. She lined up on his yardstick the French Legion of Merit, the Albanian Order of Kosygin, the Lenin Prize for ature, and a Captain Midnight Secret Decoder Ring. The lord immediately put the ring on, exclaiming happily, 'At last it came!' He instructed Nancy to file the medals and cash in the prize. He then advised her that he might not be in the next day but would keep in touch.

'Then I must have a quickie for tomorrow,' the devoted girl said flatly, 'to sustain myself.'

'Not in advance when I am in such a hurry, my dear.'

Little Nancy would not be dissuaded and, following the lord to the roof where he got into his helicopter, fell into the cockpit after him. Gently, he lowered her down on his yardstick, for he did not like his damsels getting out of hand, and zoomed off into the air.

And what did the lord find upon his return, what sight greeted him as he vaulted through the window back to the adorable Titsiepoo?

Did he find her catching up on her sleep after their many episodes? Not a bit. Was she brushing her golden tresses? Certainly not. Or searching the floor for the missing Hope Diamond? Not in the least. There she was in the arms of Blaise, revelling so hard that neither of them heard the lord come in. Suavely the lord studied the situation. His own trusty servant! And this mere slip of a girl whom he had taught all she knew, whom he had rescued from the clutches of the worst lechers in town, whom he had kept from being a newspaperwoman for two whole days to save her for higher things. But taking into account her youth and inexperience, the lord vented his full wrath on Blaise.

'You are a scoundrel,' said Lord Crinkleton.

Abashed, Blaise hung his head.

'You, sir,' said Lord Crinkleton, 'shall clean the yak latrine at my zoo every day for the next two weeks.' He didn't want to fire Blaise because he was such a good employee.

'I'd rather give up my comic books,' said Blaise, putting on a pleading look.

'My God, Blaise, why did you do it? You have your work.' The lord turned to Titsiepoo. 'And you, if I ever catch you with another man again I shall kill you.'

'Oh, my goodness!' cried Titsiepoo. 'I only did it because I missed you so.'

Charmed by her ingenuous innocence, the lord forgave his beloved. He banished Blaise to bed without supper, then made up for lost time with Titsiepoo, apologizing profusely for being away so long. And so it was that this pair, Titsiepoo and Lord Crinkleton, two people who made something of themselves, whose names are registered in the Bureau of Weights and Measurements, these two remarkable people for whom monuments have been erected, billed and cooed with molten lava kisses all through the night.

Chapter 10

'Eureka!' the lord shouted from his bath the next morning. 'I have the solution to the strawberry package.' That's how he was, this brilliant man. He pulled the rope for the footman to bring him pen and paper, and drew a diagram of a new package – just like that. He showed it to Titsiepoo who thought it very exciting, though she was not pleased that he had to go to a meeting again, especially since he had told her there were to be no other men. Tomorrow she would go and peddle her papers. She had her career to think about.

After he left, Titsiepoo sat sulking on the bed, not even bothering to put her leopard suit back on, and thinking maybe she would get a book from the lord's library in order to edify herself for her career. As she was warming up, mentally, for this assault on knowledge, someone came very softly into the room and stood before her.

It was Emerson.

The dog laid something at her feet – it was the

missing emerald necklace. 'Emerson, you darling!' cried Titsiepoo delightedly. 'Wherever did you find it?'

The happy animal stood there modestly, wagging his tail. His eyes ran over his mistress's naked body and he jumped on to the bed and lay beside her, looking up into her face from behind his horn-rimmed glasses.

'I swear, Emerson,' said Titsiepoo, 'with those glasses on you look almost like a man.'

As if to show Titsiepoo that he was indeed like a man, Emerson lay his head on one of her protuberances. Petting his furry brown head, she found it was quite a comfort to have him there. He could keep her company until the lord came back. But the touch of her hand upon his head seemed to do something to Emerson; he started to pant quite heavily, his head went to Titsiepoo's other protuberance, he stood up and looked at her anxiously, quite agitated. Then she noticed his ruler, fully as handsome as Blaise's, ready and eager to do her bidding. 'I wonder if his fur would tickle,' mused Titsiepoo aloud, and Emerson, that intellectual, that intuitive animal who knew more than so many men, that lovely dog who thought this girl was one of the most beautiful things he had ever seen, Emerson, who had been waiting for just such a sign of interest from this beautiful creature, decided forthwith to show her. Before she knew it Titsiepoo was having a new experience. The eunuchs had never told her about dogs. Emerson was indeed ardent, as ardent as Blaise or the lord himself, though somewhat different as he had no hands. However, this did not seem to matter. He made up for the lack of them by the fury of his assault, the intensity of his attention and his gratifying single-mindedness. Yes, Emerson indeed had his compensations and later, as he sat lapping her up, Titsiepoo told him what a superior being she thought he was. Just as he was about to confirm this point, his developed ears picked up the sound of the Rolls Royce upon the driveway and, with a lingering look at the surprised beauty, who had heard nothing but their quickened breathings, he headed swiftly for the neighbouring lodge where he could be sure of a warm welcome from the Scotch terrier.

Titsiepoo smoothed her glorious hair and smiled.

Chapter 11

'Did he catch him?' asked Heathcliffe the next night as Scheherazade prepared to continue the story.

'Who?'

'Lord Crinkleton.'

'Did who catch Lord Crinkleton?'

'Did Lord Crinkleton catch Emerson?'

'Well, not exactly.'

When Lord Crinkleton bounded up the stairs, four at a time, eager to show Titsiepoo the armfuls of haute couture he had bought for her, he found her stretched out on the bed clad in only her necklace. The green emeralds lay gleaming against her opalescent skin and her radiant rosebuds. The lord forgot all else for an hour or so. Finally he asked, 'Where was the necklace, my dear?'

'Oh,' said Titsiepoo, 'I found it right at my feet.'

'And where were your little feet, my love?'

'I was on my way to the library,' answered the young one truthfully.

Actually, she felt rather bad; in fact, if the truth be known, she felt a little guilty. Not that she had done anything wrong. The lord had told her not to let him catch her with another man and Emerson was not another man and besides they had not been caught. Nine times she nearly told Crinky about the incident. He might have been very helpful and of course would tell her that what she did was perfectly all right, he was such a gentleman. Nine times she refrained from so doing.

Instead she announced, 'I'm going to church tomorrow.'

'Church!' The lord looked at Titsiepoo with new wonder and amazement. Such a little saint she was. Much moved, he piled the boxes of new attire around for her to open. He helped her to try on a little orchid and black net number with removable sequins and one of the new trifles he had picked up from Tartier's: an amethyst pin in the form of a heart.

After trying on one of her new frontless nightgowns and running it up the flagpole a few times, Titsiepoo reminded the lord that she had to get some sleep in order to be up in time for church. Admiring her purposefulness and strength of will, Lord Crinkleton relinquished all holds he had upon her.

The little angel awoke at dawn and, searching among her new apparel for a dress to wear to church, she finally settled upon the one she sold her papers in. It reminded her that she must indeed get back to her job. At this rate she would never progress in her career. She was eighteen already.

So resolving, she put on the Hope Diamond, glanced at the sleeping lord, whose staff stood in readiness, and ran quietly down the stairs, careful not to awaken the devoted Emerson. Blaise was on hand and at the wheel in no time to drive her to the nearest church. 'Pick me up in an hour and a half,' she instructed him. 'Don't wait for me just in case the lord needs you.' Assuring her that the lord would not need him at so unearthly an hour, that God himself wasn't up yet, Blaise did as he was bid, devouring Titsiepoo only with his eyes because he did not wish to have his duties furthered at the zoo.

The church door was open according to the schedule posted outside but no one was attending the Mass. Figuring that the priest must be waiting in the box for troubled souls, the girl knelt before it and was about to open up her little heart when she heard a 'Bleep' and a voice announced, 'When you hear the tone it is time to start your confession.' Titsiepoo began. 'I have sinned.' There was a long pause till the voice said, 'And why did you do it, my child?' Titsiepoo burst into uncontrollable sobs.

Finally the poor girl spoke. 'Oh, Father,' she blurted, 'he wasn't even a thoroughbred!'

'Cry, my child, cry,' said the voice. 'It will do you good.' Titsiepoo cried.

'I must say in all fairness, Father, that he was very nice to me. He did behave like a gentleman. But I must not consort with mongrels, though I am sure he will expect me to and I do not want to hurt his feelings. What shall I do?'

She waited a long time for the answer, till finally it forthcame. 'First you must suffer.'

'Oh, but I have!' cried the distressed girl. 'That's why I came here. I've been suffering all night.' And the little thing cried again, her bosom heaving so in her thin dress that one of her buds worked its way through, bursting forth into the light even as a blade of grass cracks a concrete pavement in its struggle to breathe and grow.

The box didn't say anything for a long time, though Titsiepoo had her ears carefully attuned, till finally the voice asked, 'Do you repent?'

'Oh, yes, yes!' cried Titsiepoo. 'I do indeed repent, that is why I have come here. Do you forgive me, Father?'

In her eagerness to hear the answer she moved closer to the box and the voice came forth. 'Your name has been specially selected by the church computer as the winner of a contest we are running this month only to participate in a sacramental rite. Through this rite comes a cleansing of the soul and a purifying of the mind.' There was a pause during which the startled Titsiepoo wondered if she had heard correctly, another split second during which she marvelled at her good fortune, then came a loud 'Bleep!' louder than the one that had signalled the beginning of the confession, a trapdoor gave way under her, and the young penitent found herself falling through space like Alice down the rabbit hole. She bounced upon her bottom on to a cardinal red velvet spread covering a tremendous bed, so soft it must have been made entirely of feathers.

Titsiepoo looked around. The room was lit by candlelight and pervaded with the smell of sandalwood incest. It was a large room, luxurious in its very simplicity, although the furniture was dark, carved and massive.

Seraphim and cherubim flew about on the tapestries, one chasing the devil with his pitchfork and a whole group having an orgy, all beautifully done in silk thread. But the strange thing was that the room had no windows, probably because it was underground, and no visible door. Titsiepoo began to get nervous after she had looked the place over, when a figure wearing black pyjamas and a mask appeared from behind a sliding tapestry wall. 'Be not afraid, my child,' said the figure, noting the girl's startled and alarmed expression.

'Who are you?'

'I am the one appointed to perform the purifying rites,' said the figure.

Titsiepoo could not see his face but his eyes were fastened upon her in a way that not even the angels in the orgy were looking at each other. 'He couldn't be the priest,' she thought. 'He must be the sexton.'

'What are these rites?' the young girl asked. 'I really didn't seek any honours. I just came here to confess.'

'Ah, but you have won the prize,' said the sexton. So saying, he proudly displayed his organ.

Titsiepoo asked politely what he intended to do with it.

'In me,' said the sexton, 'are invested divine powers which I shall pass on to you. By touching you with my divining rod I shall penetrate your very spirit, thus cleansing you of evil thoughts.'

The little angel already had something of the divine spirit in her, however, and sensed that this man was not nearly as nice as Emerson. She sprang to her feet, an act which caused him to lose his head and make for the rose that had earlier peeped its shy way through her dress.

'Ha!' laughed the sexton, crushing her bud in the manner of a ruffian let loose in a flower garden. 'Not until I have purified you.'

Titsiepoo turned magnificently towards him. Of such scope was her sweep and of such impact that the holy man received a black eye. Then this angel, who had been taught Scriptures by the eunuchs, turned around and slapped his other. The sexton ran for holy water.

'You varmint!' he cried. 'I shall tie you to a stake, that'll teach you holiness!'

Taking advantage of his temporary blindness, Titsiepoo made for the sliding wall and pulled a rope she found there. This only set the church bells ringing. Quickly she pushed a button as the holy man reached for a towel. The door slid aside as Titsiepoo lunged forward, with the sexton behind her in hot pursuit.

'Then what?' asked Heathcliffe in a threatening tone as Scheherazade began to yawn.

Scheherazade heard the tone somewhere in her bones, and woke up.

Drawing herself up to her full height, chest out, head in, end tucked under, as she had been taught in the Girl Scouts, Titsiepoo faced her mentor. 'I have to go now,' she said. 'Lord Crinkleton's emissary is calling for me.'

At the mention of the name Lord Crinkleton, the holy man drew back as if struck. 'Lord Crinkleton!' he repeated. 'Did I hear you say "Lord Crinkleton"?'

'That is who I said.'

'Ah,' said the holy man. 'Ah!' he sang. His tone had changed, he stopped his pursuit; his mouth and eyes, the only feature visible under his mask, smiled. 'A very fine gentleman, Lord Crinkleton. Gives heavily to the church. If you are a friend of the lord, there is little I can teach you. Go, my child, be good, and may the lord keep thee.' So saying, he lit a torch and led Titsiepoo through several subterranean rooms, till they came to a staircase which they ascended. The sexton opened the door and they were in a grotto in the back of the churchyard. At their feet was a bed of fresh green leaves.

'This is where we would have finished our rite,' whispered the holy man sorrowfully. 'But you are already one of the blessed. Go, my child, and should you ever have need of the divine power vested in me, just come to the confessional.'

So saying, he was about to direct her to the path that led to the churchyard, when the bed of leaves stirred, and from it a sinuous form slowly arose.

Chapter 12

'Who?' asked Heathcliffe, for Scheherazade was giving indications of falling asleep in her chair, a neat trick she had developed.

A delicate little snore, accompanied by a kind of question mark, emanated from that lady. Heathcliffe gently picked her up and put her on the couch. If she had to sleep she may as well be comfortable so she'd be in shape to continue her story the next evening, for it was already past two.

That night the tale again unfolded.

And lo, it was a serpent who came out of the leaves. A serpent with an apple in its mouth, which it presented to Titsiepoo.

'Oh, thank you,' said the sweet young thing, and was about to take a bite when the sexton cried, 'Halt!'

Titsiepoo paused, not because she cared anything about what *he* said but because she heard familiar footsteps in the churchyard in front of the grotto. 'It's

Blaise!' she cried happily, and ran out to greet him, leaving the holy man alone with the serpent.

Blaise lit up at the sight of the lovely creature with her rosebud sticking out, apple in hand. 'Where'd you get that?' he asked, eyeing the fruit and thinking about the flower.

'A snake gave it to me.'

'You mustn't have that,' said Blaise, reaching out, 'It's poisonous.' The girl gave him the apple.

Little did Blaise know that this apple was not from any descendant of the Tree of Knowledge but had been sent by the witch who had given Titsiepoo the potion when she was fourteen. The witch was out of jail and, knowing her days to be numbered, had wanted her protégée to have an antidote should she wish it. After this act she was devoting her remaining time to concocting a wicked brew for judges.

Titsiepoo and Blaise only leered affectionately at each other, and Blaise put the apple in the glove compartment while Titsie reclined in the back seat and wondered whether she ought to mention the special rite to the lord. She and the lord had had little time to get to know each other, there were always so many things to do. The voluptuous girl sighed happily at the thought of him.

The lord was waiting for her at the lodge. 'How I have missed you, my dear!' he exclaimed. 'And how was confession?' But he did not receive an answer for the girl liked being welcomed so much that she had stepped out of the room and re-entered so that the lord could do it again. And before she knew, it was three thirty and they weren't even dressed so the lord decided to skip the board that day. And she had missed her job again. This would never do. 'I must get to the city first thing in the morning,' she said. 'I shall have to leave tonight to make sure I arrive on time. I can neglect my career no longer.'

'If you must work,' said the lord, thinking of his conversation with the monster, 'which I am against on general principle, you would do me a favour if you would mind one of my apartments that I'm not using. It's in the heart of town, very conveniently located on the corner of Fifty-Seventh Street, right next to Stax Fifth Avenue. I can open a little account for you and you can do all your shopping there.'

'Thank you,' said Titsiepoo, 'but my mother told me not to accept gifts from gentlemen. That is, to be sure, large gifts, and these sound like very large gifts.'

'My dear, the apartment will only go to waste if you do not cohabit it. As for the account at Stax', just get yourself little things like dresses and suits if it will make you feel better, and a fun chinchilla once in a while.'

'Thank you, Crinky. I shall see if I like the apartment and, if I do, perhaps I shall mind it for you.'

The lord suggested that they go and look at the apartment then and there, and that they should put some clothes on. He called Blaise to bring the Rolls and they were off in a cloud of marijuana smoke. 'It's a cosy little pad,' Lord Crinkleton explained as Blaise sped along, 'but it has large rooms. It's already decorated but you can make any changes you like.'

They arrived at the building next to Stax Fifth, a split-level ranch house on Fifty-Seventh Street. They went through the foyer lined with orange and grapefruit trees, some bearing coconuts, others guavas (botanical experiments of the lord's), to the French drawing room. 'Oh!' breathed Titsiepoo, clapping her little hands at the sight of the gold pillars supporting the frescoed ceiling where angels and cupids flitted about amidst languishing damsels and youths playing harps, and minstrels brandishing their instruments for the amusement of the damsels. Over them hovered a thundercloud in case it rained.

Lord Crinkleton ushered the ravished girl into the study, a tremendous room, with books, then off to the dining room where was ensconced gleaming mahogany furniture with a huge silver samovar on the sideboard.

On to the kitchen where sat a cook, Nanette, in a uniform, and here was also a real fireplace for roasting lambs on spits, or marshmallows.

Titsiepoo sauntered to the next level where she peeked into the bathroom, which was filled with ancestral portraits of Lord Crinkleton's father. This gentleman, known as a great swordsman even though he was only half as long as his son, died as a result of over-exertion because he could not bring himself to follow his doctor's orders about making it no more than twenty-four times a night. As a matter of fact, the lord didn't know who his mother was, his father was so promiscuous.

Next to the bathroom was a swimming pool and sauna.

The bedroom had a beautiful balcony with a sun-dial, a bird bath, plenty of chairs to recline on, and a flamingo strutting back and forth. As to the room itself, what exquisiteness! In one corner was a nine-foot-square rock garden. There were Turkish divans with a hundred pillows and gorgeous coverlets the colour of seedless melons. And a throne taken from a rajah's palace where Titsiepoo could sit and have her pedicures. A dressing table that had belonged to Marie Antoinette. Oriental throw rugs from the Occident.

Titsiepoo clapped her little hands again, a sign of delight. 'I shall be glad to mind this apartment for you, Crinky. It's very pretty.'

'Oh, Poo, I love you so much!' said Lord Crinkleton. 'Why don't we try out the divans?'

And so they did, all of them, consecrating the seedless melon-coloured coverlets with passion juice and making the walls resound with their fervent exclamations. At midnight they rang for the cook and had a slight repast of pigeon pie and couscous, and so wiled the hours away on the Oriental rugs, even the throne, until the rosy-fingered dawn goosed the flamingo on the balcony and he began to crow. 'Goodness!' said Titsiepoo, 'I must get some sleep in order to be fresh at my job. I have a big day ahead.'

'I, too,' said Lord Crinkleton. 'I am due for my ping-pong tournament in China this afternoon. Would you like to accompany me, my dear?'

'Thank you, Crinky, I must not neglect my career any more. Besides, I don't like chow mein.'

'Then I shall come flying home to you, Sweet Cookie, ere another day has broken.'

And so they fell asleep at last, two tired but happy people.

Titsiepoo dreamed of her career. And whether the lord let her pursue it is a story in itself.

Chapter 13

'He loves me,' thought Scheherazade, as she combed her hair, which she set into a new style every day now. 'He's made love to me three times. And he often comes home for dinner. What's more, he shops for it. He never used to do that. Of course, he has to, because I'm locked up.' It was difficult for her to conceive of another woman if Heathcliffe loved her. Maybe it was a problem to get rid of the other woman all at once. No, in that case he wouldn't have to kill her, he could kill the other woman.

Scheherazade had read very few murder stories, and she wasn't at all familiar with the motives. She would like to get her hands on some, they might clue her in on what was happening, but she couldn't ask Heathcliffe to get her any. He might read them and get new ideas.

She wondered if Heathcliffe still had the axe in his attaché case. He must, he kept the case near him when she was telling the story, and even when he went to the bathroom. It was terrible not to be trusted by one's own husband. Why should she go after the axe when she had no intention of using it on him? He should know her better by this time. Or should he? After all, how well did she know him? Would she ever have suspected even two weeks ago that he would do such an insane thing as come home with an axe? And for her exclusive use? Maybe they would electrocute him after he killed her! She had better tell him.

That night when he came home she said, 'Heathcliffe, dear, don't get excited, but maybe they will electrocute you if you kill me with an axe.'

'What then should I use? A revolver? They'll hear the shot next door.'

'But they will hear my screams, whereas if you used a revolver I wouldn't utter a peep.'

Heathcliffe stroked her hair. 'Would you rather a revolver?' he asked kindly.

'I think so.'

'We'll see. Did Titsiepoo get to her job that day?'

'She started out,' said Scheherazade, 'and whether she got there remains to be heard.'

'Then let me hear it.'

'Yes. But first we must follow Lord Crinkleton to China, for this was the day he was to participate in the ping-pong tournament.'

Having settled Titsiepoo in his Fifty-Seventh Street ranch house, Lord Crinkleton hopped into the space ship, specially designed for him, and zapped over to China.

A rickshaw was awaiting his landing and conveyed him to the tournament where a throng was assembled. Naturally the lord needed no introduction. Nor would an introduction have been heard, such was the uproarious greeting from the amplitudinous horde.

Lord Crinkleton took a great leap forward and in twenty-one strokes had won the game. 'Love!' he cried.

At this word a thousand damsels surged towards him. He leapt into his rickshaw, not even waiting for his medal, the damsels following after in a growing procession to his hotel. There wasn't room on the elevator for them all, so they crowded up the stairway as he was being shown to his suite. He wished to shower and nap before serving the young ladies and told them to return in an hour, but they said they must keep a united front. They planned to draw lots as to who should be first and who next. 'Why not from each according to her abilities to each according to her needs?' asked the lord.

When he awoke from his nap and went into the lounge, the number of chicks awaiting him was greatly reduced. In fact, there was only one, a Communist princess. 'Where are the others?' he asked, mildly interested.

'Oh, they had to go and fill their production quota,' smiled the princess. 'They were behind.'

The princess was very beautiful, with hazelnut eyes and a melancholy voice which spoke perfect English, although, of course, the lord spoke fluent Chinese. Reverently, he anointed her inner being. She and the lord were quite pleased with each other, so much so that he put her name down in his little red book. Then the ping-pong champion was forced to take leave of the beautiful princess because he had to stop off in Russia for a few minutes to play ping-pong there. Here the damsels were better caught up on their production quotas and seventy-five remained after the lord's nap. Since he did not have too much time, as he wanted to do a little shopping for Titsiepoo in Paris, the only arrangement he could make was to accept them into his boudoir seven at a time, where he skewered them like shashliks. The last shashlik had twelve lasses on it: they were ballerinas, among them a choreographer who said the lord had invented a new dance and invited him to join the Bolshoi.

Tearing himself away from these artists only by force of will, for they could have danced all night, Lord Crinkleton once again manned his space ship and took off for a few haute couture salons in the French capital, where he left Titsie's measurements and the wish that a few special designs might be whipped up for her. '*Mais certainement, monsieur,*' he was told. 'It ees a challenge.' Then, after dinner at Maxim's and being waylaid by several more damsels, Lord Crinkleton could tarry no longer and left for his darling Titsiepoo in the hope that she had not yet arisen and that he might one more day dissuade her from pursuing her career.

Meanwhile, back at the ranch house, Titsiepoo was indeed very much up. After serving her breakfast in bed, Nanette had somehow crept in beside the dear creature. Titsiepoo didn't quite know how it happened, she really wasn't entirely up yet because the cook had purposely omitted coffee from the otherwise full tray, but there she was with a rubber egg beater cleverly strapped to her lower torso. Her mistress was rather surprised at her employee's advances, and at first thought Nanette had joined her because she was cold. Or tired. When, however, the older woman caressed her protuberances, and there was no mistaking the ardour of her soulful kisses, Titsiepoo, who was not one to pull rank, decided to relax and enjoy her visitor. 'There is no earthly reason why you should need a man,' Nanette whispered to her, giving a clever thrust to the egg beater. 'I am far superior.' So saying, she pinched the little darling's pumpkins as though she were crimping a pie crust, and bit her on the neck. 'Be careful or Lord Crinkleton will see,' admonished Titsiepoo. 'He knows his own teeth marks.'

'Fortunately he is away most of the time during the day,' said the cook, who seemed to know something about the lord's habits, having been employed in the ranch house a while now. Bouncing upon the tender creature a few more times, and rubbing her rosebuds ever more enthusiastically, Nanette suggested that they might spend all day together, in between meals.

'That will hardly be possible,' said Titsiepoo. 'I go to work.'

Nanette looked at her as though she were crazy. 'What on earth for?' Then, quickly sensing that she had better change the subject, Nanette, who was an attractive woman, suggested in a soft voice, 'Maybe you could pick up a few things for me at Stax' and charge it to the lord's account? He'd think they were purchases for yourself and never know the difference.'

'That,' said Titsiepoo, 'would not be honest, but if there is something you have your heart set on I shall be glad to present it to you myself as a gift, Nanette.'

'Oh, never mind,' answered the cook, somewhat abashed, although a new respect crept into her voice. 'I suppose you'll be giving me your old things the way rich people always do.'

'No. I wear my things until they're worn out and I don't think you'd want them then.'

'I'd better see how the cake is that I have in the oven,' said Nanette, hurrying out. 'But,' she turned to say, 'I shall love you even though you're rich and foolish.'

Titsiepoo thought about this for a while and concluded that it was better to be rich and foolish than poor and foolish, although she certainly did not consider that she was rich; the lord was but that had nothing to do with her. 'And I am not so sure I am so foolish,' she added as an afterthought. 'However, I must see how I do in my career, it is too soon to draw any conclusions.'

As she bopped down Fifty-Seventh Street, that street of art and music where the culture of the city congregates, gentlemen stopped in their tracks, whole hordes of gentlemen on their way to Madison Avenue or to shop for naked underwear for their mistresses. Some even to look at art. Instead they all looked at Titsiepoo, for there is nothing more beautiful to look at than a working girl on her way to her job. Her little

feet, clad in golden sandals, her neat torso in a jaguar suit – the only one of its kind in the world, with hat to match – kindled the wild instincts of these artistic gentlemen. For although the lord's furrier had tailor-made the suit in classic style, Titsiepoo's magnificent proportions could by no means be subdued or camouflaged, even by a jaguar. And so it was that a number of these men, almost unknown to themselves, began to follow Titsiepoo. Whence cometh this damsel? Whither goeth she? Who was this bounteous creature sent by the wind? Thus fifty-two men, many of whom had not ridden the subways since the days of the ten-cent fare, found themselves being taken for a ride. Then up the subway steps again where Titsiepoo smiled at the sun, gave thanks for the new day, and proceeded to her news stand. A small line of diehards was waiting, extending only a little way around the corner. They directed the newcomers to the end of the line. Titsiepoo took her stand as the crowd roared.

Chapter 14

Hot foot from Paris the lord dashed into the Fifty-Seventh Street ranch house, where all he found was Nanette. 'Where is your madame?' he asked.

'She went to work.'

'To work!'

'Yes. She won't be back till a little after six. If your lordship would like, I shall serve you some tea.'

'Fine,' said Lord Crinkleton, seating himself comfortably on the couch, for it was time to think deeply about whether to call for Titsiepoo right now and take her to lunch or wait till she was finished with work. His learned brow wrinkled with the effort of concentration, so much so that he didn't even notice that Nanette had removed all her clothes when she came to serve him the tea.

He would let Titsiepoo complete her day's work, he decided. Only by working would she see the absurdity of it. In the meantime, he would bop down to the office so he gave Blaise a call. Egad, he hadn't seen

Nancy for almost two days – he had neglected her sorely. Just then his thoughts were interrupted by Nanette, who had been standing by in the hope of being more than noticed. 'May I have a charge account at Stax', sir, please?'

'No, no, Nanette!' answered the lord sharply.

'Well, I love you anyhow,' answered the cook, kneeling before the lord. On impulse, she unzipped his platinum flies and commenced to shower the contents with kisses. The lord was going to send her away at first, but kind man that he was his heart melted under this display of devotion. 'Well,' he finally concluded, 'if I don't give her a charge account, the least I can do is give her a charge,' and proceeded forthwith to do so. She was a robust girl from the country or some small town where they still had fresh air, and took to standing on her head quite easily, gasping not for breath but with excitement as the lord bestowed his favours. 'More!' she begged after half an hour. 'More, more!'

'Who are you, Oliver Twist? We must now attend to our work. I must go to my office and you must bake a cherry pie for dinner.'

'Yes, sir,' said Nanette meekly and went back to her kitchen.

Blaise was waiting downstairs and they zonked off.

'Lord Crinkleton!' Nancy squealed as the lord entered. Abandoning her typewriter, she pursued him into his office and lay down on the newly upholstered couch. 'You weren't here yesterday,' she observed.

'Ah, yes, well,' the lord replied. 'What has

occurred of interest during my absence, my dear?'

'Congress would like you to address them today, but I didn't know where to get in touch with you.'

'At what time would they like this address?'

'In half an hour.'

'Call them please, my dear, and tell them to expect me.'

'But you haven't prepared your speech.'

'I shall do it right now.' Taking out his solid uranium pen while Nancy reluctantly arose from the couch, the lord wrote out his speech forthwith, leaped into his jet-propelled helicopter and was standing before Congress in no time.

As the well-known figure entered the hall there were cheers from both parties because Lord Crinkleton was both a Republican and a Democrat. He took his stance on the podium and without reference to any notes he began:

'My friends: Unaccustomed as I am. One third of this nation. Is this a dagger? In the beginning, a spectre is haunting Europe today so that the end of all life is death. All of Gaul. Ask not. United we stand on this rock. *E pluribus unum.* I know not what course others may take but don't tread on me. Four score and seven years ago, a day that was conceived in infamy. Roll up the map of Europe and stick it in the knitted sleeve of sleep.'

The applause was positively deafening, except for those members of Congress who were so used to doing whatever the lord said that upon hearing him utter the word 'Sleep' they immediately did so. The word had a different effect upon the congresswomen, however, for three of them immediately surged forward and blew him.

Well, it was getting late, and Titsiepoo should be finishing her job soon. Reluctantly, the lord tore himself away from from Congress where he was already a member of the Hall of Fame and, mounting his helicopter, waved to the throng of spectators below. Off he went into the wild blue yonder, up, up and away. Once again, heavy thoughts wrinkled his brow. How was he going to get Titsiepoo away from that job where she met so many men? This, indeed, was a weighty matter that baffled even the lord, who was used to having the problems of the country and sometimes even of the world heaped upon his shoulders. Yet this morsel of a girl was baffling him. How was that possible? Happily, he thought about her, swerving from his course in a grand arc as he did so. When Lord Crinkleton smiled the sun broke forth upon his noble mien, lighting its every nook and cranny in a splendid array of phosphorescence reaching the very caverns of his mind, where he remembered that he had omitted Nancy from his schedule. That girl was getting the thin edge of the wedge. He would have to devise a chart to ascertain which damsel's turn it was.

As he landed, the old monstrous thought popped back into his head.

'Didn't I tell you to go?' cried the lord, who could not get over the audacity of this apparition.

'Marry Titsiepoo,' said the monster.

'Are you crazy?'

'No,' said the monster, and was gone.

'We are not going to get married,' the lord said, 'but I must devise a plan to get her away from those hundreds of men she meets every day. If this state of affairs persists, sooner or later somebody will take her away from me.' But who? He was the most magnificent man around. 'Somebody less worthy,' he thought. 'She is so young and inexperienced, how do I know her head won't be turned by some schmuck?' The lord thought on. Some time later, he knew what he had to do – he had to get Titsiepoo away from the iniquitous metropolis. Send her out to the desert. Nevada, maybe, where there were five and a half people per square mile. Let her meet one of the halves.

Even the monster turned pale at this diabolical plan. For behind the real Lord Crinkleton there lay a façade. Although he presided perfectly over all his projects he was really thinking all the time about his sweet darling.

Chapter 15

Meanwhile, back at the lodge, that scamp Emerson had returned from the Scotch terrier's and found that Titsiepoo had left. He ran around the lodge howling with frustration. Feverishly he followed Titsiepoo's scent to where the Rolls was usually parked and concluded rightly that the lord had whisked her off to parts unknown. But where? He had to see her again.

He ran up to her room, where in their haste in packing Titsiepoo's new wardrobe she and the lord had left the Hope Diamond lying carelessly on the dresser. Emerson picked up the necklace, went into the bathroom and dropped it into the toilet. 'That'll learn 'em,' he thought, flushing. Then he went into the library and read all the lord's mail. 'Who knows when he'll bring her back here?' he asked himself. 'Maybe not for weeks. Besides, I'm getting tired of living in the country. Nothing exciting ever happens.' Emerson decided that next time the Rolls came around he was going for a ride. Maybe it would take him to Titsiepoo. Blaise often came up to the lodge to study while the lord was away.

It so happened that at this very hour Blaise did indeed stop off at the lodge to get some of Titsie's things for her new apartment. On his arrival at the apartment, Nanette looked through the peephole, then opened the door with alacrity. The two of them got acquainted on the threshold, the coffee table, the couch and several other places, after which the cook brought him a plate of lasagne and a glass of red wine. 'You can come any time you have a few spare moments,' she said regarding him kindly. 'During the day is the best time.'

Neither of them noticed that Emerson was now running around the apartment looking for Titsiepoo. He went into the kitchen and in frustration ate the whole pot of *boeuf bourguignon* that was to have been the main course for dinner that night, leaving only the onions. Then he settled down to watch the couple

sporting on the chaise. Finally Blaise noticed him. 'Emerson, where did you come from? I thought I left you at the lodge.'

'He's cute, isn't he?' Nanette observed.

Emerson, his head full of Titsiepoo, didn't find Nanette too interesting, though she was a good cook. He thought they might be friends, however; Emerson believed in friendship.

'Well, I must be going,' said Blaise. 'I have to pick up the lord. You're coming with me, Emerson, though you'd better not let your master see you. He doesn't like you to be in the city where you might get run over, so you'd better lay low, kid, till we're back at the lodge.' Taking a fond leave of Nanette and assuring her he would be back anon, he departed with the protesting animal, who wished to wait for Titsiepoo.

Blaise was an unprecedented ten minutes late for the lord. Stepping into the Rolls, he bid Blaise press the rocket button that would jet them directly through the giant picture window of the board room; he did not like to set a bad example. 'If I am late so might one of them be one day and then we shall have chaos. Nay, worse. Anarchy!'

Even as he thought, the Rolls landed softly in the room. The lord stepped out and took his place at his chair. Emerson also stepped out and landed on the table. He ran up and down its full length, scanning every face as he did so. 'Emerson, you scamp!' the lord ejaculated. 'What are you doing here? I tell you, gentlemen, these animals are getting out of hand. How is a man, with his superior intelligence, going to run things, with animals acting as if they belong in our society? For it is our society, gentlemen, not theirs, make no mistake.'

At these words Emerson regarded the lord angrily. Taking up between his teeth the pen that lay beside the writing pad of one of the board members he wrote, 'The world is going to the Dogs!'

'Imperialist dog!' cried the lord.

'Uncircumcised dog,' scribbled Emerson, who had been reading Sir Walter Scott over at the Scotch terrier's domicile.

'Wrong!' exclaimed the lord, placing his pride and joy on the table defiantly.

'I should have known,' thought Emerson.

Chapter 16

After Emerson had been put into orbit in one of the lord's special satellites, the meeting continued.

'Gentlemen,' said the lord, 'I have been thinking.'

No one shouted 'Hear, hear!' for they did not wish to miss a nuance of expression on the lord's face, let alone a syllable he might utter. It was the secret wish of every board member that even a little bit of the lord's gargantuan wisdom might rub off on them, some key to his cosmic thinking, some clue to the source of his oceanic fountain of ideas. Thus there was always pin-dropping silence whenever he hinted he had a thought. 'I have been thinking, gentlemen, that the Japanese are buying up all the forests. Of course we can always get back the ones we sold them by nationalizing the forests, but then we are on the road to Communism and that we cannot have in our fair land. With the Japanese planting restaurants on every block here, not to mention trees, what a burden the white man has!' The lord's shoulders sagged for a moment, for he lived his ideas; that is why he had them.

'Therefore we shall plant forests of our own on some vast tract of land which we shall buy up for this purpose. Desert land is the cheapest, so I was thinking of Nevada. Now, of course, trees do not grow in a desert, so we shall irrigate it. Then I shall plant that forest myself. Drop seeds from a helicopter or train some birds. They'll give us a Nobel prize. When our forest grows we can sell it to the government or donate it for a tax refund and make a profit. Or maybe we'll keep it for ourselves and start a paper mill – think what a saving that would be. We could use it for printing my books; that alone is worth the investment. Why should we let the Japanese have all the paper? They will print more books and before you know it they will become more learned than we are.'

The lord had worked himself up in his enthusiasm. 'Yes, we need our own forest.' Accordingly, he proposed the resolution and it was unanimously passed. Boom. Like that.

'Next item on the agenda, gentlemen, is the strawberry package. It is on the market and sales have increased. Now we'll do the same with a raspberry package. And one of the most wonderful things about it, gentlemen, in addition to the fact that it really works, is that it holds fewer berries!'

The applause thundered out with loud clappings over the success of the strawberry package and also at the prospect of the raspberry one, so the lord held up his hand to indicate that it was enough, they must move on to other points. 'I am,' he announced, 'going to write a children's book, so we shall have a best seller on our hands. You might, during my absence of a week or so which will soon commence, wish to do some advance publicity. I don't know what it will be about yet, I may knock it up this evening, but just say it's by me. Yes, we must get into the publishing business – why should we let the poets get all the money?

'You might also give some thought while I am gone as to what berry should come after the raspberry. I have it – the gooseberry! So think about the one which should follow that.

'During my absence I may have time to paint a picture, maybe a few, if I find I like to paint, and then we shall go into the art business also. So ponder on that: where would be a good spot for a gallery, and we will kick it around when I return.

'That is all for now, gentlemen. You have a lot to think about.'

With this, he adjourned the meeting in order to tell Nancy to start making arrangements for the purchase of Nevada.

'And what, my dear, has occurred during my absence that deserves my unmitigated attention?' he asked her.

'*Vogue* wants you on its cover. Thanksgiving issue.'

'What do they want me to wear?'

'They suggested a fig leaf.'

'There are some giant prehistoric figs on the banks of the Amazon, I am told, so send someone to collect a leaf. Better make it two or three, we'll have them sewn together. Is there anything else, my dear, of import?'

'Nothing of a business nature. I brought you a present which I hope you'll like.'

'How lovely,' said the lord, before he had even opened it. It was a red velvet cushion for his seat on the stock exchange, with his coat of arms in gold.

'I embroidered it,' said Nancy modestly.

'I didn't know you were so accomplished, my dear,' said the lord tenderly, and they christened it.

A while after, Lord Crinkleton bethought himself of the damsel who should be waiting for him –

Titsiepoo – and bade Nancy a fond adieu. He found Titsiepoo reading the history of art. She was already on fertility gods.

Gently, Lord Crinkleton slipped the book from her fingers, drew the curtains on account of the damned flamingo, who liked to peek in, and they tried out a divan several times.

'I am going to Nevada for a week, my love. I'm planning a surprise for you there.'

And then he wrote his book.

Chapter 17

Before taking off for Nevada to prepare the ground for Titsiepoo's new role as Chief of Forestry, Lord Crinkleton persuaded her to go to the lodge for the weekend, although he had a hard time getting her to take Saturday off. Besides planting the forest he also planned to knock up some paintings and perhaps another children's book.

'I cannot wait for your book to appear, Crinky, saucily flanked by two covers that will house one of the tastiest literary morsels ever to accost the eye,' said Titsiepoo. 'And, may I add, all kinds of eyes – mothers, fathers and children. You will be placed among the ranks of the laureates – though, of course, you have always sat among the nightingales for me.'

The lord acknowledged her adulation with a mere nick of an eyelash, he was so modest.

'Perhaps you should write a book, for adults, too, Crinky. Like *The Memoirs of Don Juan Casa Nostra*, in which you could weave the skeins of your own life.'

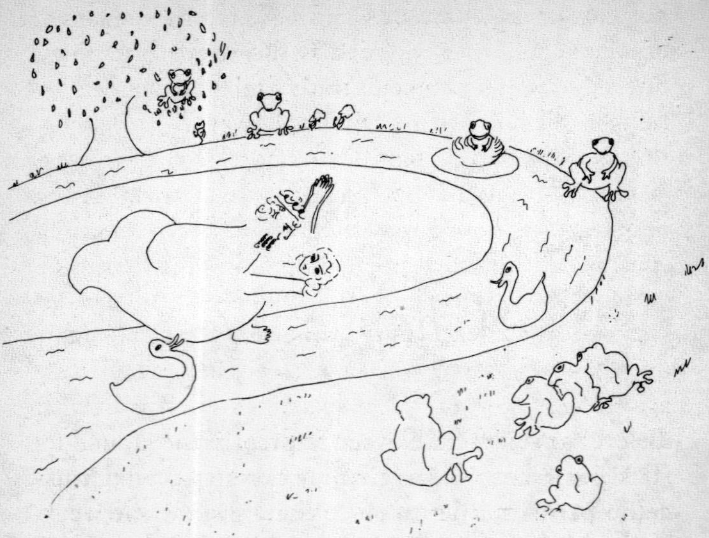

‘No, my dear. I prefer to just live it.’ And to show what he meant he grabbed her ardently, tossing her off her feet, this little critter. It is a wonder they didn’t have a fire on the bed, those two, such was the intense heat they generated, inventing things that aren’t even in the *Kama Sutra*, which they were able to do because of the extraordinary way the lord was constructed. Among these were standing with their backs to each other, Titsiepoo standing on the lord’s head like an acrobat, and the lord standing on his own head with his feet in the lotus position. Many and varied were their ways of love, sparked by their magnanimous creativity and sense of the sublime. And so they continued, not taking time out for dinner but carried ever onwards and upwards by their own unquenchable energy. Such is the strength of love. Fire did not consume it, water did not dampen it, hunger did not halt it. Finally, however, Morpheus, that jealous thing, crept down and closed their eyes. But even he could not come between them! They remained locked in sweet embrace until the morning sun peeped in, whereupon they took up where they had left off until the lord said, 'Wake! For the sun has scattered into light!' After which they had breakfast under a bodhi tree with a jug of wine, when they again made sport on the banks of a quiet stream with none but swans and frogs to watch them.

Stepping into the water they experimented aquatically, to the frustration of a passing swan who tried to get in on the act. 'Shall I let him?' asked Titsiepoo. 'I hear they are proportioned like men.'

'Maybe some men,' said the lord, drawing himself up.

So they did it again, just the two of them, and what did the lord come upon as his hands were frantically flailing at the bottom of the stream! Aha! You guessed it. It had flowed from the sewer into the ocean, thence been washed back by the waves to a river where it was borne by the wind and the rain into the quiet stream in which they now made merry. Verily, yes. It was the necklace that Emerson had caused to go down the drain, the beautiful emerald thingy containing the Hope Diamond. As the lord clasped it around Titsiepoo's slender neck and looked into her limpid eyes, he decided he must get her the Sapphire of India too, and, mayhap, to wear at week-ends, the Ruby of Omar Khayyam.

'Some of these frogs might become princes,' mused Titsiepoo.

'Never mind. I don't want you to find out. Besides, they are all bona fide frogs, my father planted their ancestors here himself on one of his multitudinous trips. It is true that one morning he found one of my mothers (we're not sure who the real one was) in bed with a prince who she said was a frog the night before. A blood test was conducted and there was no frog in him. But do keep away from frogs, even royal frogs. And besides you might get warts.' Titsie agreed reluctantly.

Back to the lodge, where the lord had a bed of roses freshly strewn for him every day, out of which magic fingers came and massaged his back when he put in a quarter. Titsiepoo said she would be glad to massage him and he could save the money. Two trapezes hung from the ceiling at opposite ends of the room for when the lord felt like flying around.

'I know what we can do,' Titsie cried, and whispered into the lord's ear. 'That is very creative of you, my dear,' he said, and they proceeded forthwith to execute her idea. Accordingly, they undressed, the lord gave her some preliminary instructions on the trapeze, and then . . . they made love in mid-air! Lord Crinkleton got on the trapeze at one end of the room, Titsiepoo mounted the other, and they met. In the beginning their aim was not perfect, for Titsie had to learn the ropes. However, she was an apt pupil in this as in everything else, and after a few hours, when the lord aimed his magical yardstick at her, she was right there. Bim, bam! What a joyous meeting of minds and hearts when those two came together, each swinging fifteen feet through the air, lingering together as sweetly and protractedly as possible, until the gravity of the swinging trapezes rendered them asunder and they swung back to either end of the room in a great arc. Wheeee! came Titsiepoo and whammm! went Lord Crinkleton. 'Glorious, my dear, glorious!' he commented. As for his companion, she could utter nothing except fervent gasps and intakes of breath, such excitement was engendered by the wild swiftness of their comings and goings together, by their ardent grabbings and mad kissings. 'My sweet embraceable you!' exclaimed the lord, to which Titsiepoo could only sigh in exchange.

'Tomorrow we will try other things on the trapezes,' promised the lord. 'Right now we'll go out and celebrate.' He took her to several night clubs, ending up at The Egret, where many of the patrons were making love under the table. 'We do not have to be subversive,' said the lord. 'We will have a go on top of the table.' And so they did, Titsiepoo standing on one table and the lord two tables away, amid the plaudits of those not occupied under the floor-length tablecloths, who mistakenly thought the ovation was for them. They continued until the wee hours, at which time the lord took the sweet thing back to the ranch house and made his departure for Nevada.

Chapter 18

'Why should I knock myself out telling you this fascinating story about Lord Crinkleton, Heathcliffe, when you are going to kill me anyway? Give me one reason why.'

'Because if you don't finish it I'll kill you sooner.'

'Okay, okay, darling.'

But before Scheherazade continued her tale she did some heavy thinking about how maybe she should try to escape after all. She had thought that life wouldn't be worth living without Heathcliffe, and that if he stuck around long enough he would fall in love with her again and not kill her – but what if he didn't fall in love with her?

'I am waiting!' broke in Heathcliffe. 'Say, how come you never told me how you met that Crinkleton character?'

'That,' said Scheherazade, 'is another story.

'The way I met Lord Crinkleton is not unusual for this great man. But what happened after that is totally without precedent in the anals of his life.

'It was many years ago, maybe twelve, and the start of the school Easter vacation. I wanted to do something extra special for the children, something mind-boggling, like taking them up the Empire State Building. So I went there early in the morning to see how the visibility was because I did not want to pay for three tickets if we weren't going to see everything. I was always so careful of your money, the way a wife should be.'

'But you were paying twice for yourself,' observed Heathcliffe.

'No, I made an arrangement with the ticket taker that I could come again that day if I wanted to. Anyway, as I was saying, I went up to see for myself because one cannot take the word of the weatherman or any of those people who do not have arthritis. So I left the children in the movies, telling them they could see it twice if I didn't return on time for any reason, and up I went. It was a nice day, with the wind to leeward.'

'How did you know it was leeward?'

'I didn't. But a man up there mentioned it was leeward and so I leaned over in order to see in which direction leeward was.'

'And where was it?'

'I never did find out due to ensuing events. The panorama from the summit of this architectural wonder was enchanting. Indeed, they have made a postcard of this very view. I feel as if I have lived recorded history when I see with my own eyes what is on a postcard. It is like being present at a presidential assassination.

'So there I was on the summit of history like Moses on Olympus, when I leaned over to see where leeward was.'

'What were you trying to do? See if it blew you away? All you had to do was wet a finger and hold it up.'

'Well, I didn't know that, my darling. As I leaned over I saw that a man was peeking down the neckline of my décolletage. I leaned further so that my head would be in his way, but alas! this proved to be too far for I fell over the precipice of this elephantine historical building and found myself hurtling down, much to the amazement of everyone who was on his way to Macy's where they were having a sale of Easter eggs and matzos. And what were my thoughts as I hurtled? That the children would be seeing Lassie Come Home five times before they realized that I might not be coming for them, and of my dear beloved husband who would be ill-prepared for my demise since he did not know how to cook. Those were my thoughts.' Scheherazade paused.

'A pretty crazy way to fall off a building,' Heathcliffe muttered. 'It's hard for me to believe that you are so foolish, Scheherazade.'

'Do you not remember Rebecca in Ivanhoe? Rebecca was going to step out of the window if the Knight Templar came one step closer. That is how it is with us virtuous women. We honour honour more than our very lives. What a jewel she was, that Rebecca.'

'He wasn't going to rape you; he was just looking.'

'Thanks. Let him look at the view he paid for. I do not go to the top of historical monuments just to provide views for gentlemen from who knows where, maybe even from New Jersey. Anyway, there I was cascading downwards, and I knew my severing of life's cord would be instantaneous. And yet, even with that realization, what filled *my mind and heart but thoughts of my beloved's image, with his eyes shining into the atmosphere. So in a way I was happy while preparing to die.*

'Imagine my incredulity then, imagine my active astonishment when, as I hurtled past the fifty-first floor, I met another leaper. Yes, someone else leapt out of the window and caught me in his arms. At first I thought it must be you, Heathcliffe, for who else would perform such a heroic feat on my account? But you, of course, were slaving away for us at your office and did not know what acute and active danger I was in. The gentleman, for what else can one call a man of such gallantry and selflessness, had the eyes of an eagle and the mind of a chess master. Because what did he spy in our downward flight but a lorry in the middle of the traffic with a load of mattresses. Using a special part of his anatomy as a rudder to steer our

course, this hero landed us right on that pile of mattresses.'

'You mean it was Crinkleton?'

'Himself.'

'The passers-by were transfixed and quickly surrounded us. But my benefactor, as if used to adulation, treated the whole thing as though it were a mere bagatelle. "Thank you, my good people," he said, "but I must tend to the lady who seems to be in need of resuscitation."

'Whispering to me that we would come back to all those nice mattresses later, the gentleman whisked me into his Rolls Royce and prodded me with a drink of brandy, first directing his chauffeur to drive far from the maddening crowd, bypassing the fire engine that was on the way, which would have arrived too late, of course, and the police car which was coming down the other block. Far from the general excitement and uproar, the reporters, the cameras, the whole bit, we drove. So we didn't get in the paper. And to think, all of this because I was so virtuous! Was it worth it, I wonder? But I suppose it was, for how else should I have met Lord Crinkleton? So you see that virtue was its own reward. For my friendship with Lord Crinkleton has been most rewarding indeed and remains one of the pinnacles of my rather quiet life.'

'Aw, come on, Scheherazade, we've had some good times, haven't we?'

'Of course, darling. And I wouldn't trade the times I've had with you for anything. But you must admit that my life has not been in the same league as eighteen-year-old Titsiepoo's. I mean, the pace is different. For instance, I have never had a dog like Emerson nor had a famous designer make me crotch suits.'

Heathcliffe squirmed uncomfortably. 'I bought you a mink suitcase once, remember?'

'Of course! Maybe we'll go somewhere for me to use it some day. I still have it safe in the vault.' She smiled dreamily. 'It will keep all my clothes nice and warm.

'Recovering from the brandy, I thanked my benefactor and asked to whom I owed my life. Bowing low from where he sat in the Rolls, he introduced himself and concluded, "At your service, madam."'

'What did he mean by that?'

'That's what he meant.

'No sooner did I recover from being rescued by this Prince Charming, than he smiled at me surreptitiously. Such was the power of his smile and such the allure of his magnetic personality that entwined itself into the cockles of my heart, that were it not for the overpowering love I had for my husband, who was dearer to me than life itself, I should very easily have been drawn in to become a member of his magic circle. And perhaps be at the hub of it, who knows? For although Titsiepoo is the hub these days, don't forget, I got there first. Twelve years ago you used to tell me I was beautiful.'

Heathcliffe looked at her slowly and carefully. 'You still are.'

'You never tell me.' She looked at him this time. Then she continued, promising herself to think about this later.

'Lord Crinkleton took my hand in his and moved closer to me. "Would you like a cup of coffee?" he asked me kindly.

'The brandy was really all I needed, but I thought it would be a good idea to go for a cup of coffee because the proximity of this magnetic man was fairly making my head

spin. But of course he had coffee right on hand in the car. He pressed a button and presto! a filigreed silver thermos of hot coffee. I was mighty glad to get it, because this man's presence was filling me with an excitement I have experienced only in the presence of one other man. Not only did he have an animal attraction, one could feel his weirdly brilliant mind exuding vitality and life-giving hormones. The vibrations were tremendous! Tremendous, I tell you, and only a woman totally and completely in love with a vastly superior husband would have been able to resist him.'

'Did you?'

'Lord Crinkleton's hand pressed mine ever so gently and some of his vibrations entered my fingers, making their way up along my anatomy. In short, my dear Heathcliffe, before I could think twice – no, not twice, even once! – I was on fire. Putting his other arm around my waist, the one that was not holding my hand, he pressed his magic lips to mine. I thought I was undone. No! Who could think under such circumstances? Certainly not most women. But I, I thought. I thought of my beloved. Resisting his burning lips I uttered a small cry. "What is it, my dear?" he asked, interested, for it is entirely likely that never before had he been interrupted by a cry like mine in the midst of such proceedings.

'"Alas, my lord," I said. "I love another."

'The lord nearly let go of my hand in his surprise. "Another?" he said. "So what? Love as many as you like, my dear, what has that got to do with our affection and esteem for each other?"

'"You don't understand. It is my husband that I love."

'Now the lord really did let go of my hand because this man, this highly sophisticated character who had been in every corner of the globe many times over and seen every stratum of society, this man had very seldom in his life heard a woman declare that she loved her husband. And if she did, it was certainly not to the exclusion of all others. So naturally he was surprised. Nay, flabbergasted. He said as much. "I am flabbergasted, Scheherazade, at what you tell me. Never in all my days have I heard true feeling expressed so truly and feelingly." That is what Lord Crinkleton said to me.'

Scheherazade paused but Heathcliffe said nothing.

'Pressing my hand again, squeezing my fingers, only in friendly fashion this time, Lord Crinkleton looked into my face. "What a remarkable woman. Marvellous!" he said. And the word "Marvellous!" dropping from his lips was like a pearl in a crystal pool.'

'Why was his "Marvellous" better than anyone else's "Marvellous"?'

'The man had style. When you say something, Heathcliffe, it is so important that it doesn't matter how you say it. But when Lord Crinkleton says something he says it with such style that it doesn't matter what he says. Which is not to say that you do not have style, but we were talking about Lord Crinkleton. To go with a piece of my tale . . . Squeezing me friendlily upon my fingers, Lord Crinkleton reiterated, "You are a wonderful woman, Scheherazade Solomon . . ."'

'How did he know your name? You never said you had told him.'

'When he introduced himself, I introduced myself,

naturally. You can't expect me to tell you every infinitesimal detail of this encounter.'

'You know the details of his other encounters.'

'More intimate details I tell. But not such details as introducing myself. Now, to resume with my resumption . . .

'After he told me again what a remarkable woman I was and similar things of this nature about my golden character and adorable body, Lord Crinkleton turned his attention to . . .'

'Wait a minute! How did he know you had an adorable body?'

'By hardly looking, it was so obvious. Adorableness stuck out all over me.

'"I should like to be your friend," said Lord Crinkleton. "It would be a new experience for me to have a woman as a friend. What a treasure you are for your husband, Scheherazade! What a lucky man is he to have someone like you to cherish! Does he know how lucky he is Scheherazade?"

'"I am sure he knows, your lordship," I answered. "Only last week he kissed me."

'"Last week! He should kiss you every day, every hour! If I were he I should never leave your side."'

'Where is he? I'll kill him!' Heathcliffe took up his axe.

'Were I not so happily married there is little doubt in my mind that I should have taken up with Lord Crinkleton. He had charisma. Not to mention chutzpah. But you already know a little about him from my previous accountants in which I have endeavoured to give you something of his flavour. But as you know, mere words cannot convey

a personality. To be in the same room with Lord Crinkleton is like watching a fireworks display.'

'Because one never knows when he's going to pop off?'

'No, silly! Because he is so dazzling. Lord Crinkleton is like one of the seven wonders of the world. However, with a superhuman effort I resisted his allure even though I am only human. And what gave me the strength for this great resistance? The thought of my dear husband! Love conquers everything. It is stronger than fire, mightier than the pen which is mightier than the sword, more enduring even than uranium which is the most durable of metals. Which is why Lord Crinkleton said to me, "You are a woman of mettle, Scheherazade."'

'Uranium disintegrates.'

'Well, while it lasts it is durable.

'And then, do you know what he did, this aristocratic man, this lord? He went down on his knees to me. Not to propose, mind you, for he got the idea of where my heart was and subtle, sophisticated people like Lord Crinkleton do not press their wishes upon others. "Do me the honour, Scheherazade," he begged, "of being my true friend."

'"Granted."

'And that is how my friendship with the great Lord Crinkleton came about, a friendship which has lasted twelve years. After the first year he announced that he could trust me with his very life, and started confiding his secrets to me, things he had told no other human being, especially not his analyst.'

'And when did this friendship end?'

'It hasn't. He probably still comes to my door but, as you know, I am not in a position to open a locked door,

and so I never answer it. No doubt he wonders what has happened to me, disappearing without a word. I'm surprised he hasn't had me traced by a private detective. He'll get around to it soon.'

'Well then, we'll have to get rid of you before that happens, won't we? Hurry up and finish your story.'

'Yes, my beloved.'

Chapter 19

And what about Emerson – all alone out there in space? He was having his ups and downs. He sustained his spirits by thinking of Titsiepoo, his love. At other times his thoughts were of Lord Crinkleton, and these were of a dastardly nature. Mostly he wondered how he could get rid of the lord so he could have Titsiepoo all to himself. Not that he wanted any harm to befall the lord – of course not! He just wanted him out of the way, like in jail or Siberia, or in quarantine for a couple of years. As his head filled with such fiendishly pleasant ideas, he felt better. Maybe he could work something out. In between such thoughts he had visions of himself playing the part of Lassie rescuing the sweet Titsiepoo from all kinds of predicaments: one time a burning house; another time, an exploding bomb; a third time, from Lord Crinkleton.

While the little beast was thinking thusly, Titsiepoo was occupied with the trunk of a tree in

Central Park, from where a beckoning finger had attracted her attention. Then a voice said, 'I've been waiting for you.' Next, a face appeared in the hollow of the trunk, the sensitive face of an artist who explained simply, in one sentence, 'I have etchings!'

'Etchings!' answered Titsiepoo. 'Oh, I should like to see them. Art is one of my main interests; in fact, it is my future career and I am ever on the lookout for both new and old works to study.' The young man, who happened to be inordinately handsome, almost as handsome as Lord Crinkleton, helped her into the tree, and there indeed, hanging inside the tree, were etchings second only to Goya. 'What a find!' exclaimed Titsiepoo.

So delighted was the young man at her appreciation and so happy was Titsiepoo at her first art discovery that they fell into each other's arms and were soon in total eclipse. Fortunately it was a very large tree, a giant redwood, so it was able to accommodate them quite comfortably.

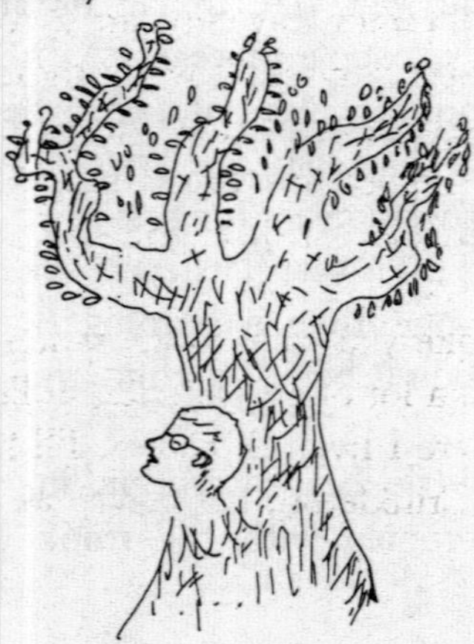

'Nice place you have here,' said Titsie, looking around when the two of them had unlocked themselves, for it was evident that the artist either lived here or used the place as a studio, since it was lit with seven-and-a-half watt bulbs.

'Yes,' he answered. 'I like to be close to nature, and what is more natural than a tree? Especially a tree who intimately lives with rain.'

Titsiepoo clapped her hands. 'You are a poet, too!' she cried. 'What is your name? I must remember you.'

'I'm Arthur King, but my friends call me Art.'

'May I call you Art, Arthur?'

'You bet. We are friends.' So saying, he gave the little angel a friendly squeeze and soon the giant tree shook with their revelations. Although Art did not have a yardstick, he had a paintbrush, and he did wonderful things with it, such as giving her sweeping brush strokes all over until she felt very artistic – abstract, even, since there was no paint on the brush. Indeed, Art expressed her feelings by saying, 'You are my painting and I must leave no part of you undone. I don't like empty canvases.' With these words, he painted her rosebuds until they turned from pink to crimson, then dipped his brush into his paintpot. Titsiepoo's shrieks of joy got lost among the treetops.

'I'd like to take you back to my ranch house,' she said. 'There are a lot of art galleries on Fifty-Seventh Street near where I live. Of course, I'll have to hide you from Lord Crinkleton, but maybe we can arrange something.'

'You must get some practice in hiding me, so let's go there now,' said Art. So off the two of them went to the ranch house, oblivious of time and its vast importunities.

Hand in hand they sauntered, making plans for Art's paintings and etchings to be shown. 'Maybe we will hang some in Stax Fifth Avenue,' said Titsie. 'I live next door.'

After this heavy conversation they took a little respite in bed, during which Art became busy on the little angel with his paintbrush, using new and modern techniques along with some of his classical training. Thus were they occupied when Art's pointy ears, developed by his living so close to nature – nay, right inside it – heard the lord's approach.

'Don't worry,' said Titsiepoo. 'Hide on the balcony.'

The lord bounced in, all smiles, with the official offer for Titsiepoo to become Chief of Forestry of the State of Nevada. The lass was surprised and pleased by this offer but said she needed time to think. 'It is not exactly in my line of experience,' she observed.

'No, my dear, that is why it is so good. It will broaden your horizons and also give you time to take correspondence courses in the history of art or whatever you like.'

'I shall consider it, Crinky dear, and thank you.'

That is how the lord was to Titsiepoo, always consulting her wishes, always letting her do as she wished and trying to make her happy, and that is why she remained faithful to him for so long when typhoons and artists, as well as intellectuals like Emerson, were after her.

'Faithful? She wasn't faithful!' exclaimed Heathcliffe.

'She was still with him, and look how far I am in my story. She didn't have to stay with him, a girl like that. She could go live in a tree with Arthur King. Or with any of her customers, many of whom were rich and powerful. The mayor himself would be glad to get such a girl, not to mention several movie magnets and captives of industry. And look at all the time she gave him. A girl like that should be in the limelight with her name up in beacons.'

'But he's such a catch!' said Heathcliffe.

'Who said she wanted to get married?'

'Oh, I thought she wanted to.'

'Why should she be so different from him?'

'Hmmm.'

Chapter 20

Heathcliffe Solomon did not ordinarily go around accompanied by an axe. He had never been violent, had never so much as slapped his children down when they were small and irritating. Raising his hand to Scheherazade in their twenty-eight years of marriage would have been unthinkable; they had always used their voices in a quarrel. Nor had there been too many of these. And here he was with an axe.

'Am I doing the right thing?' he asked himself. The answer had seemed so obvious before. His Uncle Max, who had brought him up, had tried to teach him that things are not always black and white, that there are shades of grey, but Heathcliffe had never wanted to accept this. 'They are either right or wrong,' he had always said. 'It's like being a little bit pregnant. You either are or you're not.'

'No,' said Uncle Max. 'Right or wrong can be like the story of the beard. At which point does a man have a beard? First he looks as if he needs a shave, then people

say, "Oh, you're growing a beard." Then they say, "It's coming along nicely." When do they acknowledge, "That's a fine beard"? Another hair, another quarter of an inch can make the difference.'

Good old Uncle Max. Uncle Max hadn't finished grammar school, had taught himself to read and write when he came to this country, and had gone on to make a mint. His home was lined with Persian carpets, his table groaned under the weight of fine food. He had taken Heathcliffe and his mother in when she and his father had been separated. His father had come to see him once a month, at which time Heathcliffe would hide or refuse to go. He much preferred his uncle.

Uncle Max's children had not been nice to Heathcliffe; they weren't at all like their father. His ambition in those days had been that when he grew up he'd show them; he'd have as much money as Uncle Max. Yet the good man had never taught him that money was important. 'Always be nice,' said Uncle Max. 'If the other fellow is a louse, don't you be one. Be nice to him, then he'll feel bad.'

The years passed, Uncle Max died, his sons fell into his money and never saw Heathcliffe. And Heathcliffe hadn't been able to show them yet what a success he was. 'That's because I'm not playing my cards right,' he told himself. 'As soon as a good hand comes up for me, I'm going to play it. They'll hear about it, too. I'll see to that.' They would hear about him the same way he heard about them, that they weren't as well off as they used to be, that they weren't as sharp as the old man for all their degrees in Business Administration and who knew what else. 'Maybe they'll lose it all,' Heathcliffe dreamed happily, 'and they'll *come to me for a loan. And I'll say, "Oh, yes, I remember you. You and your brother never let me play with you, told me I wasn't part of the family. Why don't you go to him for a loan? Or to someone in your family?"' Or maybe he'd fool them and be nice, Uncle Max style. 'Sure,' he would say to them, 'how much do you want? Any time. And don't be ashamed to come to me again.'*

The time had now come for him to play his cards, and he didn't exactly like the hand he had been dealt. He knew he had to play, yet even if he won, he lost. The choice was between promotion and being out of a job. However, the promotion was for a single man, that was the only kind the company would accept, to keep the medical coverage at a minimum. 'Forget the medical coverage,' said Heathcliffe.

'I can do without it.' 'No,' said Personnel, 'company policy says we must provide it.'

That is how matters stood. How could he be single unless he divorced Scheherazade? He couldn't divorce her until he made more money in order to pay for the divorce and alimony, and he couldn't pay these until he had a better job. It was a vicious circle with no exit.

The alternative was unemployment, which in these days of big former executives driving taxi cabs and glad to get such work, amounted to total annihilation. 'I'd wind up on welfare,' thought Heathcliffe. 'Scheherazade deserves better than that. I couldn't stand that for her.'

And so he had begun bucking for the promotion, staying in the office till all hours and taking work with him in his briefcase to pore over in the train. He had been doing this for months now, working so hard and seeing Scheherazade so seldom that he had almost forgotten what she was like. 'Lord Crinkleton is right,' he said, 'she is a wonderful woman.' How could he let her live in poverty? It would be better if she never had the experience, better if she had a short life and a happy one. He was going to kill her for love. He was sure he was doing the right thing – and yet he put his head in his hands and sobbed. 'Oh, Uncle Max,' he said. 'if only you were here to tell me what to do.'

Chapter 21

The day after his arrival back in the Big City Lord Crinkleton decided to go to his job, so he got up early – noon. 'My word,' he ejaculated, 'I forgot to do my paintings. I thought I'd be away longer. I'll have to do some this week-end if I get a few minutes. I promised the Board. But I have my children's book, that is something to get them started on; they can set up a publishing house, and they have all the berry packages to work on and maybe we will do something with nuts. I know what should be on the nut packages! A picture of a squirrel. And we will start a fashion of squirrels as pets, that should sell a lot of nuts. Every squirrel who wants to get fed will have to become a pet because there won't be any nuts left for him to eat otherwise. And maybe we will have the image of a bear on the berry package. A cub, of course, and everyone will get a cub as a pet. Only I don't know what we'll do with them when they grow up. We'll have to take that up at the Board. Ah, yes! Opportunities for expansion are limitless in this great nation.' So saying, he turned to the sweet Titsiepoo and gently grabbed her, whereupon they had an assignation, for they had not had one since the previous evening, the lord being too fatigued from his journey and Titsiepoo from her bout with Arthur to awaken several times during the night as was their wont. Wantonly tossing the blankets into the air while the lord exclaimed over the marvels of her pudendum, Titsiepoo abandoned herself to the pleasures of love.

When the two had torn themselves asunder, Titsiepoo remembered that she had to make Art famous. The newspaper business would have to wait, she decided, because Art was more important. Accordingly, after the lord had made his departure, she jumped into an exotic little badger dress and made her way to Stax'.

Drawing herself up haughtily as befitted the future Chief of Forestry, Titsiepoo demanded to see Mr Stax.

'We don't just barge in on Mr Stax,' explained the girl at the desk. 'We make an appointment, sometimes a week or two in advance.'

'Tell him it's the Chief of Forestry of the State of Nevada.'

'The Chief of Forestry!' repeated the awed girl. 'The Chief, you say?' she murmured, wanting to make sure she had heard aright, for she had not been trained to think a chief could look anything like Titsiepoo.

'The Chief.'

'I shall see if he's available.'

'Maybe I should accept the post,' Titsiepoo said to herself. 'I am exactly the same person I was before I was informed I am the Chief, and look how differently she treats me. However, if people are so silly as to be impressed by a title they don't deserve for it to be authentic.'

Before too long the girl returned and led Titsiepoo to an upstairs chamber.

The great merchant, Henri Stax, lay upon a chaise longue in his exquisite office where a grandmother clock ticked softly and a few Renoirs decorated the walls. Mr Stax looked about a hundred but was probably only eighty. Still, he could not get up from his couch. 'Lie down, my dear,' he invited.

'Thank you,' said Titsie, 'but I am here on business. I have come to show you some etchings and paintings you might like to exhibit in your fine emporium.'

'Etchings!' exclaimed the great Mr Stax, making room on the chaise. 'Here, I have moved over. Show me.'

Titsiepoo opened a portfolio and pulled out Art's work which she proceeded to show one by one. Finally she came to one Art had done of her.

'These are very fine,' said the great merchant. 'I will buy that one.'

'Would you like to exhibit the others in your great emporium?'

'You would do better in a gallery,' said Mr Stax, reaching out to the lovely lass. 'I will call my friend Marvel at the Nonesuch Gallery, I am a good client of his. He will give your friend an exhibition.' So saying, he stroked the hair of the lovely Titsiepoo whose eyes closed in ecstasy until she resembled some gorgeous cat, whereupon Mr Stax proceeded quietly to remove her clothes as if he thought she would not know what was going on because she wasn't looking. 'What a pretty little thing you are,' he whispered, gazing reverently at the largest passion fruits he had ever seen in all his eighty-two and a half years and taking a bite. At this, Titsiepoo opened her eyes and asked him what he was doing. 'Nothing,' he answered, stroking her hair again. 'Go to sleep.' And so the afternoon wore on, Mr Stax stroking the girl in all her soft and secret places and she, mesmerized, having been completely taken by surprise since she had not expected a gentleman of his advanced years to take such an active interest in things of the flesh. Mr Stax had not even a ruler, his organ was little more than a letter opener, and a refined one at that, the kind that would grace a lady's kneehole desk. Nor did he seem able to do too much with it except wait for Titsiepoo to yawn when he would eagerly shove it into her mouth. So grateful was he for these small favours, and so pleased with the girl, that she not only tolerated him as an act of charity but even grew fond of him as one might of a grandfather in the Old Testament. Laying his head upon a soccer ball while its rosebud stole up into his ear, pleasantly tickling it, Mr Stax said, 'Now I shall call Marvel. Not only will he like your pictures but he owes me something.' Saying which, Mr Stax regretfully arose from the chaise to make the call, whereupon the little angel opened her eyes fully, put all her clothes back on and reassembled her portfolio.

'It is settled,' said Mr Stax, all smiles, having concluded his transaction over the phone. 'Your friend will be in the Nonesuch.'

'But doesn't he want to look at the work first?'

'It doesn't matter. I have told him it is very fine.'

'Oh.'

'And now I will pay you for this portrait. How much is it?'

'I don't know. I hadn't thought about it yet.'

'That is not the way to do business, my dear girl. You must put a price upon your wares or decide what the traffic will bear. Here,' and taking out a stuffed wallet made from garter snakes and tooled with only his name, 'Stax', he pressed a generous supply of its contents upon her. 'See Marvel in the morning. He expects you.'

'Oh, Mr Stax, how wonderful!' exclaimed Titsiepoo, planting a kiss upon his forehead. 'Arthur is launched.'

'Not yet,' said Mr Stax. 'I shall buy another picture at the opening and then others will buy. Then he will be launched.'

'It seems very easy for an artist to be launched.'

'No, it is not usually easy,' said Mr Stax, 'but you are a marvellous agent, my dear. It is all your doing. And you must visit me again. Perhaps we will launch some other people.'

Titsiepoo did not tell the great Stax that she lived right next door to him, since she expected to be going to Nevada and there was no point in promoting the friendship which had begun so auspiciously. 'I will see you at the opening,' she said gaily, 'and thank you for all your help.'

'Not at all, my dear, not at all. Any time I can render similar services do not hesitate to call upon me.' Saying which, Mr Stax sank back upon the chaise, for it was a long time since he had spent such an active afternoon. 'Forgive me if I do not see you to the door, my dear.'

Kissing the top of his head, Titsiepoo took her

departure. 'So Art is launched,' she told herself happily. 'Now I just have to find him a place to live.'

But that problem, too, was not desperate, as she found upon her return, for there was Arthur waiting for her. He had found himself another tree in Central Park where he had spent the night. 'It's so conveniently located,' he said, 'near you and right in the centre of town. One couldn't ask for anything better.'

'I think we *can* do better,' answered Titsiepoo. When she told him the news of his launching he was more than delighted. 'This calls for a celebration,' he said, pulling her into the bedroom. Titsiepoo kept her head.

'Be gone,' said the little darling, 'for his lordship will be here momentarily. Only tell me which tree I can find you in after I see Mr Marvel tomorrow so that I can tell you all that transpires.'

The eager Arthur never told her, however, for at that very moment the voice of Lord Crinkleton was heard in the flat, inquiring of Nanette what she had made for dinner. Leaping out on to the balcony, Arthur made his way along the ledge to the building next door, where he climbed through an open window and landed in the office of the great merchant, Henri Stax.

Chapter 22

'What,' asked Henri Stax, rising from the chaise where he had been resting; indeed, he had not the strength yet to zip his flies, 'what are you doing in my office?'

'And what,' said Arthur King answering a question with a question, 'is my painting doing in here?' For his eye had alighted upon his portrait of Titsiepoo which stood out in such prominence where it had been temporarily propped against the wall.

'I have purchased that painting, young man. What makes you think it's yours?'

'I painted it,' replied Arthur.

'Ah, so you are the artist,' said Mr Stax pleasantly. 'I have just arranged an exhibition for you. But what are you doing here?'

'I was looking for a place to live. One near here.'

'Well,' said Mr Stax, 'you can sleep here tonight, only be out by nine in the morning because I have to occupy my office. Perhaps Marvel can help you find an apartment. He's your agent and agents often help with such things. After all, an artist has to have a place to work. Where have you been staying?'

'In a tree.'

'A tree! Hah! Most unique, my young fellow. I dare say you would like some privacy then, so I shall go and leave you to your own devices. My private bath is in there,' Mr Stax said, pointing to a door, 'and you may use my robe. I am sorry I do not have sheets for you, I never spend the night here, but there is a coverlet I usually use for my naps. Make all the calls you want but have no visitors in my private office, and let me know how you are getting along for I shall not see you in the morning; you must be out of here by then. Tell Marvel I said to help you and you will be taken care of.' Before he departed, Mr Stax zipped up his flies and offered Art a glass of brandy. Art looked around the lavish office and gave a low whistle. 'It is more comfortable than my tree,' he observed, 'and right next door to Titsiepoo. I can visit her any time the lord is out just by climbing through the windows. However, the lord is out only during the day and I am not allowed here then. I must find a way to evacuate old Stax and have this place for myself.'

'Jesus!' interjected Heathcliffe. 'You didn't tell me he was such a rat.'

'Of course not,' said Scheherazade. 'That can be divulged only as the story unfolds.'

Art helped himself to a cigar, one of Cuba's finest, for of course Mr Stax, the great merchant, had his own way of getting forbidden merchandise. The cigars were stamped 'Made in China'. He sat in the leather upholstered swivel chair, leaned back as far as it would go, and put his feet up on the desk. He eyed the French blue telephone nestling among the many neatly arrayed objets d'art and called his friends all over

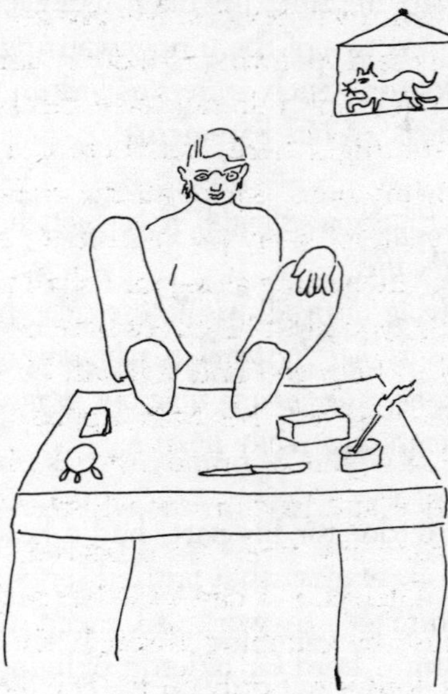

the world. He helped himself from the box of fine chocolates he found at his elbow, till they were gone. Then he turned his attention to his painting. 'Hmm,' he thought, 'if Stax likes that painting so much so will a lot of other people. I shall paint some more exactly like it and distribute them in different towns.' Pleased with his idea, he leaned back and thought some more. 'Maybe I can find a quick way of doing it, too, like taking a photograph of the painting and then painting over the photo. In fact, anything I sell I'll copy.' He got up and helped himself to Mr Stax' liquor supply. 'Wish he had some food here. I'll fix all that up when I get rid of him and move in. And Lord Crinkleton,' Art continued with his wicked thoughts, 'wanting Titsiepoo all to himself. I'll have to evacuate him, too.' So that was two of them now wanting to get rid of Lord Crinkleton. Such secrets as lurk in the hearts of men and dogs! What basements!

'Art and Emerson should have gotten together,' observed Heathcliffe.

'Are you giving them ideas? Whose side are you on?' Scheherazade cast her husband a withering glance and continued with her tale, taking time out to make a pot of tea, for his remark had really upset her.

Lord Crinkleton, for his part, had a hard first day back on the job. Nancy, that faithful servant, did not want to let him get to work, so eager was she for favours from him. Lord Crinkleton obligingly tickled various parts of her anatomy with his yardstick until she was reduced to a quivering mass of errata. 'O, lord, how I missed you,' she breathed. Finally, wrenching himself away, Lord Crinkleton inquired what had occurred of interest during his absence.

'Oh, quite a lot, my lord. To begin with, the Department of Defence wants you to address the generals on How to Achieve Peace Through War.'

'Accept. What else?'

'The Psychological Convention wants you to address its members on Penis Envy.'

'Accept. Book them both on the same day. We'll take up other business later, I have to go to the meeting now. By the way,' he inquired kindly, 'what have you been doing while I was away, my dear? For fun, that is?'

'I tried the paddle of a canoe but it was no substitute for you.'

'I should think not. Which end?' Without waiting for an answer, the lord was off.

Chapter 23

Ingmar Marvel stood looking gloomily at the passers-by out of the second-floor window of his Madison Avenue gallery. He often thought of jumping out of the window, not because business was bad – it wasn't – but because he was Swedish. His eye wandered over the marvellous paintings that lined the walls and the sculptures that stood away from them, and he was bored. Because he was Swedish. He held his head in his hand. 'Why couldn't I be something else?' he hollered to the paintings. 'English, maybe?'

Thus he was carrying on, holding himself back from jumping out of the window, as he did at least once a day, when the door opened and an angel walked in. Titsiepoo. Carrying many paintings. 'Stax sent me,' she said simply.

Mr Marvel walked over to Titsiepoo, removed the paintings from her hands and looked at her without a word.

Titsiepoo, of course, was used to men becoming

speechless at the sight of her and stood there waiting for him to recover. He seemed to be taking a long time.

Finally Ingmar Marvel spoke. 'Yes, Mr Stax called me yesterday about some artist you discovered. I shall look at his work presently. In the meantime, have some sherry, my dear, and tell me about yourself.'

'This is my first discovery,' said Titsiepoo, glad to talk to someone about her ambition, for Lord Crinkleton did not seem to encourage it. 'I am thinking of becoming a museum curator.'

'Most interesting, darling,' said Mr Marvel, his sombre eyes alive with an unaccustomed light as they took in the full scope of her singular anatomy, 'but why?'

'For Art's sake.'

'And how will you go about becoming one, my darling?'

'I shall study. I have almost enough money to stop working, and I shall make discoveries. Unless I switch to teaching. I should like to teach kindergarten.'

'I could hire you to work in my gallery, you would learn a lot here, but, then, who would look at the paintings?' muttered Mr Marvel. 'My advice to you, darling, is to switch to kindergarten, though I do not know what the parents will say when their five-year-old boys pubesce.'

'Working in your gallery would be a wonderful opportunity, Mr Marvel.'

'I think not, my dear, for the reason I have stated. However, feel free to visit me any time and we will talk and I will try to teach you things.' To demonstrate his good faith, Ingmar Marvel took Titsiepoo into the storeroom where stacks of paintings were stored in bins and pulled a few out to show her why they were important. And then a funny thing happened. Gazing at the lovely Titsiepoo whilst she was regarding the paintings, his interest in life seemed to return! He felt alive again! To hell with window-jumping! Seizing the sweet lovely by the waist he buried his head in her soccer balls while he tried to pull her dress up with only one hand.

'But Mr Marvel,' said the surprised lass, 'you said you were going to teach me things.'

'I am.' He shook his head in the affirmative. 'Nice things.' And before the sweet Titsiepoo could protest both of her arms were out of their sleeves and Mr Marvel had laid her gently on the long counter on top of the bins that stored the paintings. His ruler, though one inch short of twelve, made up for this deficiency by the uniqueness of its shape. It was curved like a scimitar. 'You might think I am Turkish, but I am not,' he explained, noting the question in the lass's eyes. 'Somewhere, some time, no one knows how or why, I had a French ancestor. This is called "The French Twist". Elegant, is it not? There are not too many of them.' Without waiting for her to answer as to whether it was elegant, he placed his scimitar in the deep and lovely valley of her soccer balls and almost swooned at the sensation he encountered. Carried away, and screaming softly, he pressed the twin mountains around himself, lifting her from the counter and standing her before him while he peered down in adoration at her little angel face, which looked at him questioningly. That was his undoing, for it distracted his attention and he did not aim carefully, since his scimitar caught under her chin and the force of his thrust sent the little angel hurtling heavenward. 'OOps!' shouted Ingmar Marvel, genuinely concerned. 'Sorry about that. Are you hurt?'

'No,' Titsiepoo managed to gasp from her position, supine upon a painting of the Mother and Child before Mr Marvel lay prone and full upon her and proceeded to get lost again among her mountains. 'We must be careful, darling,' he said, this time paying more attention. 'I wouldn't hurt you for the world.' 'Ow! Ow! Ow!' screamed Titsiepoo as he bit her neck. Back and forth Ingmar brandished his scimitar in the mountain pass while he kissed and caressed her rosebuds which stood to full attention until he showered them with his dewdrops of desire. 'Not for the world.'

'And now we will look at the paintings,' he said merrily, helping Titsiepoo back into her sleeves. 'Haven't you forgotten something?' she asked, for she considered that he had but begun. 'Oh, yes. Tell your artist I shall book an exhibition in six weeks. These are very fine indeed. In the meantime, darling, visit me as often as you can and we shall talk about Art.' He gave her a deep look out of his brooding eyes and she quivered like a blade of grass before a storm. Such was his power over her.

'I do not know,' she quavered.

'I command you to come!'

And Titsiepoo – came! She forgave him everything.

They held each other by their glance till finally Titsiepoo nodded. 'He commanded me!' she thought as she left. 'That is what I shall do when I am Chief of Forestry – command people.' For now that Art was launched it was time to think about assuming the duties that had been offered to her. But she would wait till Art's exhibition. That would be an astronomical event she really must attend.

Mr Marvel advanced some money for Arthur. Marvel was always advancing artists money. One artist was in hock for his next two hundred and twelve paintings.

'Perhaps Mr Marvel would help you find a place to live,' Titsiepoo suggested innocently to Art.

'I'll be all right in my tree, I really will. Besides, I have a lot of painting to do and don't have time to move around too much.'

Titsiepoo, too, had a lot to do, and most of all she felt the call of her news stand. An uproarious cheer went up from the patient lookouts at her approach. Men threw their hats into the air in excitement at sight of her and did not care if they landed on heads other than their own. Thus are new fashions born and proceed from class to mass. And, as birds spread the word, until the snow is black with their little bodies eagerly pecking at crumbs, so in no time had a line of men formed of such proportions that extra police had to be summoned.

'Oh, my goodness,' said Titsiepoo. And the thought crossed her mind that she was really of use right here, making people happy. Why, then, go elsewhere to be a chief? Well, she wouldn't be leaving until after Art's exhibition, so there was plenty of time to think.

So many notes were pressed upon her that afternoon that Blaise had to bring giant plastic garbage bags in which to put them. She would look at them all that very night, for she did not like to get behind in her reading.

While she was thus occupied making the population at large so happy, Lord Crinkleton was otherwise engaged. He had to address the generals. 'To the top of the Sixes, Blaise,' he said, and sat back deep in thought inside his artistic head. Upon their arrival he was greeted by a group of surly pacifists blocking the sidewalk to picket the generals. Using his seventh sense, Lord Crinkleton leapt out of the Rolls just in time to deactivate a bomb with his yardstick. And then the action began. For another group of militants wielding machetes attacked him, coming, as it seemed, out of nowhere. Again the lord used his yardstick, first as a vaulting pole, then duelled their leaders whom he vanquished in no time with it. Springing up on the soap box, the lord shouted, 'Peace, gentlemen! Peace at any price. And those generals upstairs are going to bring it to you – after they win the war. Only think, without war, the word "Peace" wouldn't mean anything. There could be no anti-war movies, no peace movement. Peace, brothers and sisters. Om shanti. Peace. Long live war.'

After this, the lord felt complete fulfilment of himself, his art, and peace, and went up to address the meeting whose members had been watching him out of the window and applauded him so vociferously even before he had said a word that he had half a mind not to speak. And so that is what he did. And they got the message. He then took off in a blaze of not inephemeral glory to address the Psychological Convention on the subject of which he was the world's undisputed authority.

Chapter 24

Arthur wanted to be big like Lord Crinkleton. And not just anatomically. He wanted to be so big that he'd be called King Arthur instead of Arthur King. He would begin by making a lot of money from his art. He would take over the establishment of that illustrious merchant, Henri Stax . . . how he didn't quite know yet. He would get rid of that man of highest fame and esteem, Lord Crinkleton, and take over Titsiepoo. He didn't quite know how he would do these things, either – one thing at a time. Right now he was busy making many copies of the portrait of Titsiepoo Mr Stax had bought, to distribute among the smaller galleries that ringed the great metropolis. It would have been just as easy, would it not, for a man of his talent to paint new and original ideas. But Arthur King wanted a sure seller. And so he began this heinous crime of copying himself right in the office of that genuine art lover, Mr Stax. In the mornings, when he had to leave before nine, he took a bus or train and visited the galleries on Long Island or in Westchester. He had no trouble placing his work, it was so outstanding.

His benefactress, in the meantime, was in blissful ignominiousness of the fact that this would-be king was a shit, and was happily making so much money at her small emporium that one morning she had to put her heaps of coins and stacks of dollars into an armoured car with two guards sitting in the back pointing their guns at each other. Not to mention the many jewels that men were always pressing upon her. But she liked the jewels Lord Crinkleton gave her most and put the others into a vault.

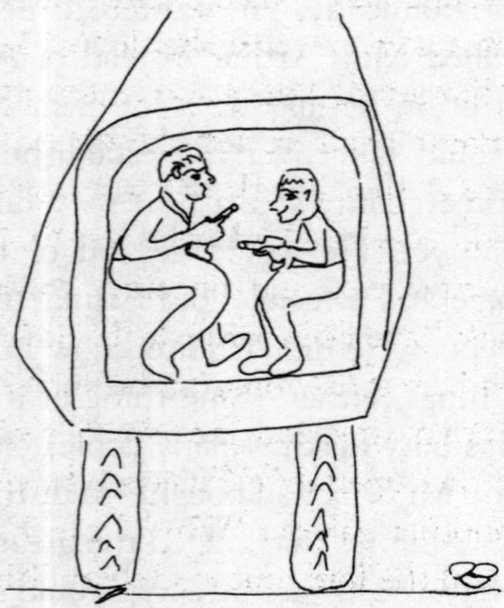

Ah, foolish Arthur King for thinking he was so smart! He had not counted on Lord Crinkleton's moving in mysterious ways. How could he know that the lord was in the process of looking over some of the galleries the Board had suggested he buy up?

One morning Lord Crinkleton bestowed a visit on the Nonesuch. 'Egad, Marvel,' he said, 'I haven't seen you in such good spirits for a long time. Anything wrong?'

'No, but I am all right anyway.'

'Say, Marvel, what do you think of this?' And the lord showed him one of his paintings on which he had blocked out his initials, 'J.C.', in order not to influence opinion.

'Splendid!' said that fine dealer and connoisseur, Ingmar Marvel, who knew so much about painting that he couldn't paint. 'But what a coincidence. This ravishing young lady you've painted was up here with some paintings by an artist she discovered only a few days ago. I'm giving him a show next month. Come see his things.' And he led the lord into the store room where Arthur's work was waiting.

'Not bad,' said the lord, who saw in a flash, that man of perspicacity and uncanny wisdom, what a thrill it must have been for little Titsie to have discovered so fine an artist. Imagine his further shock that very afternoon to come face to face with another portrait of the superlative Titsiepoo by the very same artist in another gallery! 'Why, I can hardly believe my eyes!' said the lord, out loud. 'And King signed up to let Marvel represent him exclusively. Marvel will have to hear about this, I am afraid, or his gallery will get a bad name. How am I going to break the news to him that I saw a King hanging in Westchester? It will give Marvel an excuse to hang himself!'

If the lord was surprised to see the King painting in Westchester, he really lost his composure when he saw the very same portrait of Titsiepoo in a gallery in Long Island. 'He's done two of them!' he roared. Of course he didn't know about the one hanging in Mr Stax' office or the five that were in other galleries. But he had seen enough.

It would be redundant to say that Mr Marvel cancelled the exhibition. 'Too bad,' he said. 'That chap has ruined a brilliant career. Man's greatest enemy is man.'

'Especially when that man is himself,' the lord added.

Of course Mr Stax heard about Arthur's expulsion, too, from Marvel and was quite upset that there were copies of his Titsiepoo portrait. He had a speech all prepared for Arthur next time that young man had the effrontery to show his face in his fine establishment. The gods were frowning on Arthur. They sent a policeman looking into his tree where he was sitting quietly, eating bananas. 'I've been watching you,' the officer said, 'and you've been living here. We don't want any punkos in the park!'

Arthur was arrested for vagrancy and when his trial came up Lord Crinkleton was sent for. That gentleman divulged the more serious crime Arthur was perpetrating. 'He is un-American,' the lord stated flatly, 'and could easily corrupt other artists. This bad apple should be thrown out of the barrel, gentlemen. In short, he should be deported.'

The Soviet Union offered to take Arthur provided

he agreed to paint socialist realism. His first work was a sculpture for the Kremlin: Lord Crinkleton and Titsiepoo, even larger than life, looming above the heads of the people like two Slavic gods, holding aloft the hammer and sickle. Small copies for home use found their way on to the black market.

Chapter 25

'You are no longer needed,' Lord Crinkleton announced to the monster. 'I am going to marry Titsiepoo.' A lovely smile spread over the monster's face and he changed from dark blue to pale mauve. 'What convinced you?' he asked.

'The Arthur incident. My little angel has good judgement about art but she is still naïve about people. Imagine if she had been in a position of authority and had chosen such a person. She could have utterly ruined herself. She needs my protection.'

'That's something new,' said Heathcliffe. 'Before he wanted to protect her from his rivals. Now he's going to further the career he didn't want her to have.'

'He was against her having a career because he was afraid she'd meet other men. Actually, he was very proud that she had the ambition to do something worthwhile as long as he'd have her all to himself. He didn't want her off in Nevada either; he wanted her at his side always.

'So he made up his stupendous mind to take the plunge. It was just at this point that Titsiepoo announced that she was ready to give up her newspaper business and start studying art history full time.'

'A wise idea, my dear,' Lord Crinkleton said, 'to give up your business enterprise that you have been unmitigatedly enslaved by and to prepare for something higher. However, there is something even more exalted I am going to suggest to you.'

The sweet Titsiepoo answered, 'Oh, Crinky, you are so ineffably wise and full of sagacity. What I need is to absorb some of your wisdom.'

At these words, which took place in the Rolls, the lord dismissed Blaise, telling him to return in three hours, and pressed the seat-lowering button. He would propose later. The two assumed many positions, including some that had never been assumed by anybody since the world began, not even by birds in flight.

When Titsie's happy hollers had subsided, she said, 'Blaise will be returning any minute. Why don't we put on our clothes while we wait for him and continue at my place, Crinky?'

'A good idea, my dear. And I am hungry, are you?'

'No. But Nanette can whip you up something.'

Blaise was late, which would not have bothered the lord were he not so hungry. Opening the glove compartment in hopes of a candy bar, he found only the apple that Blaise had stopped Titsiepoo from eating some months ago. Titsiepoo was busy putting her

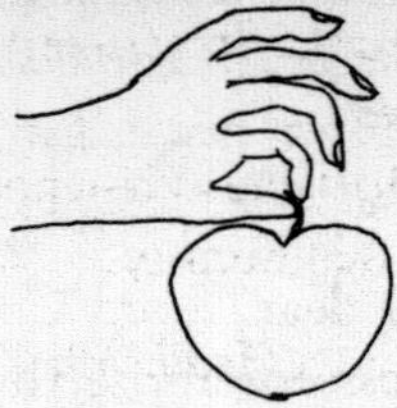

shoes on and did not notice what the lord was up to. Lord Crinkleton took a bite of the perfect fruit and let out a shattering howl. Titsiepoo looked up in horror, for it was not the kind of cry she had ever heard emanate from anyone, let alone from Crinky's lordly throat. She stared at him, not able to believe that it was he who had uttered the cry.

Lord Crinkleton looked as though he had just seen Medusa. He could not move. He could not speak.

'What is it, what is it, Crinky darling?'

Crinky did not answer.

'Speak to me!'

Lord Crinkleton must surely have been turned to stone for all the reaction Titsiepoo got from him. His expression of horror remained fixed.

Titsiepoo looked at the fallen apple and something connected in her mind. She remembered the apple that the doctor of philosophy did not want her to eat, though she never knew why. She looked from the apple to the lord and he shook his head in confirmation. And then . . . oh, then he showed her a sorrowful sight. He unsheathed his yardstick; Titsiepoo tried to stifle a cry, but too late. It escaped her, not so loud as the lord's had been, but unmistakably one of horror. For something had happened to his precious implement. It had shrunk. It was only half its size. A mere eighteen inches.

That was the one time Titsiepoo ever saw Lord Crinkleton lose his equanimity.

'I should think so,' said Heathcliffe. 'Did it make much difference to his life style?'

'Not really. After all, even at eighteen inches Lord Crinkleton was way out front. But everything is relative and the lord considered that he had suffered a great loss. He felt as if he wasn't all there.'

As for Titsiepoo, she loved him anyway, even though she had claimed that she was interested in only ONE THING. And the proof was that she asked him to marry her then and there because she knew that now he would never ask her.

'I thought she wasn't interested in marriage.'

'She wasn't, but she didn't want the lord to be insecure.'

'Alas, my dear, I am only half my former self. I am not good enough for you!' he remonstrated sadly.

'I love you for your soul,' she answered. 'And your mind,' she added. 'There is always your mind, which we must not overlook.'

'Imagine if I had taken a bigger bite of that wretched piece of fruit,' he shuddered. 'Or if you had been hungry and I had offered it to you first.'

'It was intended for me. The witch must have sent it in case I wanted it.'

'Then I am glad I ate it, my dear, for I should not want anything foolish to happen to you.' Fiercely, Lord Crinkleton clasped the sweet Titsiepoo to his macho chest and with his mere eighteen inches managed to make her very happy indeed.

'Well,' said Heathcliffe, 'he had wanted to put her in a velvet cage from the moment he saw her to keep her all to himself. Yet she managed to find the ace of knaves. What alternative did he have but the one he hadn't tried yet – to marry her.'

'Oh, Heathcliffe, you're so brilliant.'

'No, I'm not really, Scheherazade. You'd be surprised at all the important things I know nothing about. People, for instance. That's my trouble; I know too little and too much.'

'Well, why don't you just reverse them?'

'What?'

'Try not to interrupt so much, darling. I'm nearly through with my recount.'

'Nearly through? Say, I'm going to miss those two. I almost wish you weren't finished; they have become so interesting to me.'

'But you kept telling me to finish so I have hurried as much as I could. And now we are nearly at the grand finale.'

'Too bad.'

Scheherazade gave her husband a funny look.

Chapter 26

The associate curator of the Metropolitan Museum of Art said out loud, 'This is all very well but the Louvre is larger. We shall have to move to France.' Who was this curator who spoke thus? Lady Crinkleton. Thus she spake while combing her golden tresses in between appointments in one of her many offices. Appointments! Did I say 'Appointments'? Usually they were assignations.

Who knows all the rooms in the Metropolitan? There isn't enough space on the floor plan. Besides, Lady Crinkleton had had some rooms especially built in secret. All but the one she now stood in had a chaise longue like Henri Stax'. One had a sliding wall like that she had fallen into with the sexton, another had trapezes as she had seen in the lord's lodge. Sometimes she used one of the store rooms as Marvel did; other times she ran outside with her escort into a hollow tree like Art's. As I have stated many times, she was an apt pupil.

'The little minx!' exclaimed Heathcliffe.

'Not really,' said Scheherazade. 'One cannot call Titsiepoo surreptitious or even subliminal. She just didn't want to hurt the lord, for she remembered what a jealous thing he was with the Blaise episode, so she doesn't expect him to change.'

'Has he?'

'He has indeed. Whereas he had wanted to put her in a gilded cage, as you have so astutely observed, the one who gave up his freedom was himself. He became faithful; what is more he enjoys it because he feels as though he is making the ultimate sacrifice for love. He feels noble, virtuous and sublime. The more sublime he feels, the more self-sacrificing, the more he loves her for making him feel so sublime.

'Their roles were reversed. She doesn't seem to know about fidelity after marriage, never having given it a passing thought. Not that she doesn't love and adore him. So full is her nature, however, so giving and spontaneous, that she also loves a few thousand other people, angel that she is. She has become a female Crinkleton.'

'And that's no angel.'

'To him she is.'

And so we bring to a close the true story of Lord Crinkleton and Lady Titsiepoo, two of the great amours of all time, synonymous with Héloise and Abelard, Orpheus and Eurydice, Dick Tracey and Katherine Hepburn, Mrs Thatcher and Ronald Reagan. These two have crept into the minds and hearts of the populace and have taken their place in the hall of history. That is living proof that the American people have good taste, except when electing a President. They knew that these two were great. And they aren't even dead yet.

'How did Nancy feel when the lord got married?'

'Oh, she married Blaise. Keeps the records of all his PhDs because he still works for the lord and has lots of time to study.'

'And Emerson?'

'He's with them after his splashout. To this day the lord doesn't know about some of his many qualifications. Well, that ends my story.' Scheherazade looked squarely at Heathcliffe, who had a strange expression on his face. Frightened, she asked, 'Would you like to hear another?'

'No,' said Heathcliffe, rising. 'No. Because I am going to kill you.'

'A wonderful, magical novel'
MARION ZIMMER BRADLEY

The Finnbranch

·PAUL·HAZEL·

From the wintry land of the mountains came Finn, the warrior whose legacy was both a blessing and a curse.

His mother was a witch and a wanderer upon land. His father – from what they knew – had risen up like a god from his kingdom beneath the sea.

And so Finn began his odyssey in search of his birthright: drawn deep into the secret world of sorcery, braving waters that would drown a man in dreams, roving among people who would answer riddles with fresh riddles . . .

'Dark and intriguing, at once wonderful and strange . . . one of the best fantasies in some time' Publishers Weekly

0 7221 4545 4 FANTASY £4.95